THE DRAGON'S BRIDE

A DEAL WITH A DEMON NOVEL

KATEE ROBERT

TRINKETS AND TALES LLC

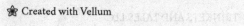 Created with Vellum

To Jack Harbon. This book wouldn't exist without His Beauty imprinting on my very soul. Thank you!

CONTENT NOTES

*P*lease be aware that some content in this book may be trigger for some readers. Reader discretion is advised.

TROPES: Marriage of convenience, monster romance

TAGS: demon bargains, I only watch Once Upon a Time for the scaly lizard man, beauty and the beast retelling, soft monsters, two peens, size difference, falling for the monster husband you never wanted, forced proximity, if you sexy run I will sexy chase you, breeding, you're too big, mating frenzy, sorry not sorry I accidentally on purpose ripped off your birth control pendant

CWs: domestic abuse (historical, off-page, but the heroine is dealing with the aftermath of getting out of that relationship), murder (off-page), human/non-human sex, size difference, explicit sex, breeding, light choking, injuries for blood magic, small incidental injuries, pregnancy (epilogue), birth (epilogue)

CHAPTER 1

BRIAR

Three days ago, I didn't believe demons existed.

Now, I'm signing a contract with one.

Life comes at you fast.

My body is one large, throbbing bruise as I try to focus on the words swimming before my eyes. "I don't want to do this."

"I'm aware. People don't make deals with me unless they're desperate." The demon doesn't look much like a demon. Then again, what do I know? Maybe all demons are handsome, dark-haired white guys whose shadows don't quite line up with their bodies.

I press a hand to my head. My brain feels like it's sloshing around inside my skull. "How did you even find me?"

He shrugs. "Desperation has a certain flavor. One of my people happened upon you last week and brought you to my attention."

Last week I was doing my best to covertly arrange an escape route that my husband Ethan wouldn't know about until it was too late. The plan had been to flee while he was at work and disappear without a trace. I thought I'd had every factor accounted for, but I was so damn scared.

I'm still scared.

"I thought I was getting out." It feels very naive to say it now. Three days ago, I'd laughed in this stranger's face, had been determined not to put myself under the control of another man—human or no. Who comes knocking on someone's door in the middle of the day, offering a *demon deal*? Apparently Azazel does. It was all so normal and yet strange, but how could I worry about this alleged demon when my personal monster was so much closer to home and more dangerous?

I was getting out. Or so I thought. That was before Ethan managed to figure out what hotel I was staying at. Before he came here and... I shake my head, which only makes the nausea worse. "It's very likely that I'm concussed. This kind of deal won't be binding in court."

Azazel's dark gaze tracks to the right side of my face. I've seen what I look like. Bruises on top of bruises, which doesn't make sense because Ethan only hit me once before one of the other hotel guests came running down the hall and stopped him. A good Samaritan who probably saved my life.

Next time, I won't be so lucky.

I close my eyes and take several slow breaths. It doesn't help, but I'm not sure anything can help right now. I'm out of options. *Desperate*, as the demon says. Maybe if I had family to run to, things would be different, but even if I did, I'd just be endangering them as well. I could go buy a gun, but I've no faith that I'm capable of murder, let alone that the justice system would land on my side. All their grace seems to be saved for the predators themselves.

"Would you like me to read it to you?" I don't think this demon is capable of sounding soft, but he's gone quiet in a way that makes the small hair at the nape of my neck stand on end.

I open my eyes to find him still staring at my face. Even as I tell myself not to, I lift a hand to press against the swollen skin around my eye. "I'm sure that would be convenient for you. You can leave out whatever you want."

He sighs, an almost imperceptible sound. "Deals are sacred, Briar Rose. I'm willing to play dirty leading up to them, but there are no tricks in the fine print. It's in everyone's best interest that my...clients...go into things with their eyes wide open."

The horrible feeling of there not being enough air in this dingy hotel room gets worse. "Did you tell him how to find me?"

Azazel narrows his eyes. "I didn't have to. He knew about your secret credit card. After you left, he tracked the charge to this place and sweet talked the front desk girl into giving him your room number. He told her he wanted to surprise you for your anniversary."

I don't ask how he knows that. He seems to know a lot of things he shouldn't. I stare down at my fingers, nails bitten down to the quick. A horrible habit of mine, one that's only gotten worse in the last few days. "Rookie mistake."

"Fear makes fools of us all."

He's not exactly being nice, but he's not being particularly pushy, either. I slump back in my chair and motion at the contract. "Go ahead, then." It's not like I have much choice. I'm going to say yes, and we both know it. In this moment, I'm barely holding it together, my strength so brittle that if he pushed, I'd fold in an instant.

Azazel plucks the contract from the desk and moves to perch on the edge of the worn-looking bed. He glances at me and then begins to read. It's nothing more than I expected; he'd already laid out the details three days ago.

Seven years of service to be paid up front before he does what *I* need. A bargain entered into willingly, in which I won't be forced to do anything I don't want to do. I laugh at that clause. There are a lot of ways to ensure someone's obedience without "forcing." It's the reason I'm in this mess to begin with.

"Wait, say that again."

Azazel pauses. "If you become pregnant, the child will not return with you to this realm upon the completion of your contract."

I stare. "You left that out when you went over the offer last time."

"I didn't want you to get the wrong idea."

The wrong idea. Right. Nothing about this deal seemed too good to be true, but there was an element of wondering when the other shoe would drop. Now it's dropping hard enough to make my head spin. "So that's what this is. A breeding program."

"I am merely covering all bases."

I don't believe him for a moment. Obviously, I was aware sex may be part of the deal. Azazel looks human enough, even if I get the feeling it's a convenient form to hold and not necessarily his real one. The thought almost makes me laugh. Amazing how quickly the human brain can adapt when there are no other routes left. "And if I don't want to have sex with anyone?"

Again, that unreadable look flicks in my direction. "As I said, you will not be required to do anything you don't want to do. You will, however, give the person of my choosing the opportunity to seduce you."

So many layers to that sentence. I have absolutely no reason to trust him, but I'm also out of options. Still, I can't help stalling. Just a little. "Why seven years?"

"Magic is a strange creature." He shrugs. "Certain things

amplify it and allow for the impossible. Numbers have meaning. Seven, in particular, is powerful in all the realms. So we bargain for seven years."

That doesn't really make sense to me, but nothing makes sense to me. In the end, it doesn't matter. I don't have any other options. "Give it here."

Azazel passes over the contract and produces a pen from somewhere, likely his perfectly tailored black jacket. The paper is thicker than I expected, almost a vellum. I can't quite stop myself from rubbing my fingers against it. "Only the best for demon deals, I guess."

I don't give myself time to think, to let my mind run through the maze filled with my anxieties. I'm damned if I do, damned if I don't. I have no money, no family, nowhere to run where Ethan can't find me. He's made it damn clear that the next time he gets his hands on me, I won't survive the experience.

Signing my name on this contract might be opening myself up for an even worse outcome. I'm not naive enough to think there's nothing worse than death, but it's still preferable. Maybe Azazel will keep his word. Maybe he won't.

At least Ethan won't live to hurt me or anyone else again.

In seven years...How many people will he hurt in the meantime?

"What about..." I don't have family. All my true friends drifted off within the first year of my relationship with Ethan. I hardly call being forced to be cordial with *his* friends' wives being actual friends. We don't speak outside those uncomfortable dinners. Still. I swallow hard. "Disappearing for seven years will raise some questions."

"You won't be gone for seven years." At my confusion, he exhales slowly. "Time moves differently in the various realms. It's not entirely consistent, and we bargainer demons can be a little selective with manipulating things, but seven years in the demon realm is anywhere from an hour to a few months here, depending on a few factors."

I blink. "So I'll appear back here in an hour or a few months, but seven years older." What a way to waste a life.

"No." A sharp shake of his head. "The aging process is..." Azazel makes a frustrated motion with his hand. "It has to do with the magic steeped in every atom in my realm, but even humans who reside there live longer than they do here. You won't be immortal, but if you were to spend the rest of your life there, you'd likely live a hundred and fifty years at least. You will age over these seven years, but not at the rate you would in the human realm."

It all seems too convenient, but it's not as if I have any choice. If Ethan is tracking my secret credit card, he'll find me quickly no matter where I go. I *have* to take this deal.

I swallow my fear and sign with a shaking hand. The moment the pen tip leaves the paper, something foreign sizzles through me. I gasp and press my hand to my chest.

"The magic of a binding contract." Azazel rises and waves his hand at the desk. Shadows surge from the edges of the room, and the paper disappears. He adjusts his jacket. "Under normal circumstances, the payment comes first before I fulfill the terms of the contract. However, I'm inclined to make an exception this time."

"What?" Surely he's not saying what I think he's saying?

His gaze narrows on my face. "Don't get any noble ideas. You're merchandise now, Briar, and that means your husband has damaged what's mine. Beyond that, you don't seem the type to be unfaithful, and I'd rather not leave any loose ends to damage *my* end goal."

Before I can ask him what the hell *that* means, he vanishes in another surge of shadows. My skin prickles with sheer terror, but my body is too tired to do anything about it but shake. Maybe I'm in shock. It wouldn't be surprising, considering everything that's happened today.

I slump back in the chair, and a hysterical giggle slips free. "The demon didn't even want my soul. How disappointing."

Seven years of service.

Such a long time, and yet no time at all. I spend fifteen seconds considering what I might do when my sentence is served and I'm free of both Azazel and Ethan. My mind shies away from thinking about it too hard, almost as if allowing myself to dream will jinx it.

I stumble to my feet and cross to the bag filled with all my worldly goods. I don't know how long Azazel is going to take, and I'm practically weaving on my feet at this point, but I don't dare shower or sleep. He hasn't done anything to harm me, but that doesn't mean I trust him.

In the end, I only have enough time to take some ibuprofen before the shadows gather at the corner of the room and peel away to reveal the demon. He looks...different. I blink, wondering if my head injury is the reason it seems like he has horns for a moment. I blink again, and the feeling passes.

"Time to go." He wipes at his hands with a handkerchief, but it's not quite doing a good job of cleaning away the red stains there. He catches me looking and shrugs. "Sometimes I feel like getting my hands dirty. I'm sure you understand."

The sickeningly swimming feeling comes back, even more pronounced this time. "Is that..." I have to stop to catch my breath. "Is that *Ethan's* blood?"

"Of course it is. I hardly go around committing murder for the fun of it." He tucks the handkerchief into the inner pocket of his jacket. "Though all you humans are rather breakable, so sometimes accidents happen."

I don't know how to process *that* any more than the fact I can still see the bloodstains on his hands. Hands that seem to...flicker...the longer I watch them. Pale skin and then deep red and then pale again. I press my hand to my temple, but this conversation has been one shock too many. "I think I'm going to pass out," I say faintly.

The room gives a sickening spin, and then I'm falling.

Azazel was all the way across the room from me, but he still catches me before I hit the floor, scooping me up into arms that feel far larger than they appear. "Can't have you killing yourself with another blow to the head."

I try to speak, I think. Maybe to protest. Maybe to thank him for doing what I'd never be able to do on my own. In the end, it doesn't matter. A deep blackness surges up and swallows me whole.

CHAPTER 2

BRIAR

I wake up in a strange bed. Instinct takes over, and I
lie perfectly still, eyes closed and breathing even.
It's a nice bed, the mattress below me strange and soft in a
way that seems to invite lying down and never getting back
up again. The blanket over me is lightweight but more than
keeps the faint chill of the room away. It slides against my
skin decadently as I shift.

My *bare* skin.

Where the hell are my clothes?

"You can stop pretending to be asleep, Briar."

I recognize the voice even though it's only been a few
days since I met him. *Azazel.* I sit up—and have to bite back a
scream. The voice is the only thing about him that's the
same. I look around the room for some other explanation.
Surely the broody-looking demon who made the deal with
me isn't this giant, horned, crimson-skinned beast sprawled
in a chair on the other side of the room?

My brain skips, shudders, and goes numb.

This is fine. It's better than the alternative. I take a breath and then another. On the third one, I no longer sound like I'm about to hyperventilate. *Good. This is good.* "Azazel."

He studies me out of dark eyes that might look different than the ones I was familiar with, but the sardonic amusement at my expense is the same. "You're taking this rather well."

"Hysterics aren't going to change anything."

"Hmmm." He sits forward and flicks his fingers at one of his horns. "I only wear my human form when I'm in your realm. Now, we're in mine, and there's no need to do so."

I'd listened to the offer, had allowed him to read the contract to me. Somehow, in all that, I hadn't really processed that other realms existed, let alone that I'd be traveling to one. It feels too big to comprehend, so I focus on something else. "Where are my clothes?"

"They'll be returned to you when your contract is fulfilled, along with your other personal effects."

I look around the room, mostly to give myself time to process that. I don't have much worth fighting over, but the photos in my suitcase are the only ones I have of my gran. "They'll be kept safe?"

"Yes."

I have no reason to believe him, but this isn't a fight I'm going to win. I don't know if I've *ever* been in a fight I had a chance at winning. Without thinking, I press my hand to my face. It's only then that I realize the throbbing pain is nowhere in evidence. I prod my skin gently, but the swelling seems to be gone as well. "How long have I been out?"

"A few hours. Transitioning from realm to realm isn't easy, even when you're traveling with me." He pauses until I look at him. "A healer took care of your injuries."

"Oh." I drop my hand. "Thank you."

"You're one of my bargaining chips for a better future. It's not in my best interest for you to be bloodied and broken on the auction block." He pushes slowly to his feet, which is right around the time I realize how massive he is. He's got to be seven feet. He's *got* to be. "There are dresses in the wardrobe. One of them should suit. You have an hour." He turns and walks out of the room.

I stare at the door for a long moment, processing what he said. *Auction block.* I'd honestly thought he meant to keep me for himself, but apparently that isn't the case.

Does it really matter? There's not much you can do about it now.

A gibbering terror threatens to break through my artificial calm, but I muscle it back. If I start crying now, I'm going to end up curling in a ball and sobbing until I can't breathe. And nothing will change. If I'm supposed to be auctioned off, I won't know anything about the person who purchases me until it's over. Azazel has promised I won't be forced or come to harm, but how far does that promise extend when I'm outside his control?

Movement has always helped. It keeps my fears from freezing me. Hopefully that will continue to hold true.

I fight my way out of the ridiculously plush bed and, after a short argument with myself, wrap the sheet around my body and pad to the wardrobe. It's built on the scale of Azazel, so I have to reach up to grab the handle and wrestle the heavy door open. Inside, I find a rainbow of garments. Some of the textures I recognize, some I don't, but they all seem horrifyingly expensive. I drag my fingers over the soft fabrics and worry my bottom lip.

Of course they're expensive. Azazel is *auctioning me off*. I should probably be grateful he's not going to put me on the auction block naked and weeping. The thought makes me shudder, and I grab a dress at random.

It's not the most complicated design, but it's got a corset kind of bodice beneath my breasts, and it takes a lot of cursing and twisting to get it in place. I gather up the long skirt and walk to the massive ornate mirror angled near the door.

I look…

I stare blankly at my reflection. Gone are my favored oversized sweatshirts and loose jeans. The white dress clings to my waist and ribs, the structure of the bodice making my breasts look much larger than they are, pressing them up until the ruffles of the top seem to cling precariously to their slopes. The skirts aren't as billowy as they feel, draping down to brush the tops of my bare feet.

Reluctantly, I lift my gaze to my face. The swelling is gone, of course. But more than that, this *healer* has done something to me. My skin has never looked so dewy and unblemished—not even when I was in my early twenties. And my hair…

I should have cut it. It's too red, too wavy, too *noticeable*. The years and lack of care had dulled it, which in turn helped to keep other men from looking at me; something that infuriated Ethan even though it's not as if I solicited attention ever. My hair isn't dull and frizzy now. It looks like I've just come from some spa and salon treatment.

I don't look like *me*.

A quick exploration of the rest of the room reveals a cleverly understated door that leads to a bathroom. It takes a bit of experimentation since nothing looks quite like I'm used to, but I am *deeply* relieved to discover they have indoor plumbing in this realm.

I barely get back into the room before the large door Azazel left through creaks open. I freeze, but no one appears. Seconds tick by into minutes before I'm able to make my body move. Even then, it's a fight against myself to walk to the door and peer out. "Hello?"

The hallway is twice as wide as I'm used to and well over

ten feet tall. It stretches down to a corner where it turns right, and there are a number of side tables arranged against one wall and four doors between mine and the turn.

The other doors swing open without a sound. I tense, ready to scramble back into my room and slam the door, but then a woman steps out of the nearest door. She's nearly as pale as me and has an athletic build that's a little on the soft side. Her brown hair is piled on her head and her dress is deep blue and short, hugging her curves. She turns to look at me, and I distantly note that her nose is crooked.

On the other side of her, another woman steps out. This one is tall and lean with a light tan. She wears a slinky purple dress with a slit up one side. Her black hair falls around her beautiful face in waves, but the way she looks around isn't as confused or tentative as I feel. She looks like a soldier about to go to war.

Next is a curvy woman with light-brown skin and thick dark curls in a ponytail. She's wearing a deep red gown that clings to her breasts and billows out about her. She looks at us and laughs, the sound bright. "Wow, we look good."

Through the final door tentatively steps a woman in yellow that shows off a round and soft body. Her blond hair hangs in a shining bob, and she seems utterly terrified, her pale features completely colorless.

The woman in purple studies us for a long moment and shrugs. "Might as well get this over with." She turns and starts down the hallway.

Herd mentality kicks in, and we move as one to follow her. Or maybe no one wants to be left alone now that we've found others. Aside from the woman in yellow, none of them seem quite as freaked out as I feel beneath the fragile layer of calm I'm barely holding on to. I don't know if that makes me feel better or worse, so I set it aside and fall to the back of our group to give myself some time to process.

The woman in red chats happily, not seeming to care that she's only getting monosyllabic responses. The one in purple who's leading the pack seems to pick up her pace, and I can't tell if it's an attempt to distance herself from the rest of us or because she's hunting something. Her stride is predatory, and if she were coming at *me* like that, I'd turn around and run for my life.

The hallway ends at another door. The woman in purple doesn't hesitate. She wrenches it open and stalks through. The rest of us exchange a look, and then the woman in red moves to follow. One by one, we file through the door after them. Low lights make it challenging to see, but not so much that I miss our destination.

A dais at the front of the room.

One by one, we step up and form a line. It's a little brighter here, which only makes it more challenging to see the rest of the room. I get the impression of large shapes but not details.

I *do* recognize Azazel's voice, though, when he says, "Now, we make our selections."

CHAPTER 3

SOL

$\mathcal{I}$ expected this auction to be a trap. The demon realm might not currently be at war, but we're never far off. Skirmishes happen along borders as a matter of course, and occasionally those escalate to larger conflicts. Not recently, but...

The fact Azazel has managed to convince all four leaders to come here is a feat in and of itself. Maybe they're just as desperate for the power he can dole out at a whim as I am. It's not a comfortable thought. My life would be significantly easier if I married one of the eligible dragon women in my territory. If I wasn't the territory leader, that's exactly what I would have done. There are plenty of lovely women in my own territory who I could have been happy with. Perhaps we'd even have children at this point.

Unfortunately, my responsibilities to the greater good means when Azazel dangles the possibility of a human bride in front of me, I have to leap at the offer. There's nothing *wrong* with humans, but attending this auction, allowing myself to pick a bride provided by a bargainer demon, puts me in a precarious position.

I know how bargainers work. Each of these five human women will have entered into their contracts willingly. Azazel might be a right bastard, but he can't shake the intrinsic truths of his flavor of demon. The contract reigns supreme.

No, Azazel is too invested in the long game to be an immediate threat tonight.

Not like Rusalka lounging only a few feet away, fire flickering beneath her smoky skin and her long tail twitching rhythmically. She looks at the women with a hunger that has me fighting not to hiss. Nothing good comes when the succubi go hunting. What is this auction if not a hunt?

On the other side of her, Bram has his wings tucked tight against his body as if he expects an attack at any moment. His claws keep flexing at his side, and from the way he glares at Rusalka, he hasn't forgotten that a few short years ago, only a last-minute intervention kept their territories from going to war. I doubt he's been this close to her in decades. An opportunity, though the cost is too high for any of us to risk it.

Hopefully.

Azazel and his people are the only ones who can cross to the human realm. Generations ago, the veils between realms were thinner, more easily breached at certain moments. It was never *easy*, though, not with time moving differently in each realm. Only the bargainer demons can manipulate that factor, and even then only to a limited degree. Still, it was possible for others to cross at will.

No longer.

The faint sound of water has me half turning to keep Thane in my line of sight. He's hardly at his best here in a tub that barely contains his tentacles, but I've grappled with him enough to be wary all the same. He might not be able to drag me to the dark depths, but he can restrain and strangle someone without drowning them.

I haven't had cause to frequent the bargainer demons' castle recently, and I'm not surprised to find it still unsettling in the extreme to have hallways shift around me and doors appear on walls that were previously blank. It's an excellent defensive spell, sure to have any enemy trapped within the walls until the bargainers can deal with them, but I get the feeling it changes at a whim simply to fuck with the people who move through the space.

Stone doesn't move. Stone is steady and reliable and completely and utterly *unspooky*.

It's an effort to keep my crest from flaring in response to the threat all around me. I'm no youngling. I've ruled long enough that being in a room with the four other most dangerous leaders in our realm isn't enough to get to me.

The risk is high, but it's worth it. The bargainers guard their contracted humans closely, and though those humans are occasionally allowed to *entertain* themselves with guests of Azazel, those encounters are always restricted. In hindsight, it's a brilliant move. He curated a taste, a temptation, a possibility that only he can fulfill. Now, he'll do so...for a price.

If it were only sexual, I could have ignored the invitation to this auction. Sex with humans is enjoyable, but hardly worth risking my entire territory to acquire in a permanent way. Azazel's too canny to offer that. He's baiting the trap with so much more. Our bloodlines once mixed generously with humans. It wasn't until the ability to pass between the realms became impossible for the rest of us that we realized what we'd lost. At least those of us *not* among the bargainers.

Rusalka shifts forward, her eyes flaring red. "I want the one in red."

Azazel doesn't move. "And agree to the treaty and payment in return."

"Yes, yes." She waves that away. "I'll sign the contract. Don't get your horns in a twist."

"I'll take yellow."

Azazel gives a sharp shake of his head. "Pick another."

Bram rumbles a little, his wings flaring as if he'll challenge the bargainer demon, but he finally shrugs. "They're all the same to me. Purple."

"Very well." Azazel's grin goes knife-sharp for a moment before he turns in my direction.

I exchange a look with Thane. These women might be all the same to Bram, but I'm partial to the one with bright red hair. It's an eye-catching color, and with the way she stares out at the room despite the fact the lights must hide most of our details from view, she doesn't seem afraid.

Truth or lie?

There's only one way to find out.

"Why offer the yellow if you're going to keep her to yourself?"

Azazel stares down at the kraken. "I have my reasons. Pick another."

"Blue." Thane moves in his pool, tentacles shifting over each other beneath the water. The ones on his head—where the humans have hair—are mostly behaving, though there's a nod to his tension in the way they slither over his shoulders, moving in a wind that doesn't exist.

I don't quite exhale in relief, but the temptation is there all the same. "White."

"Perfect." Azazel claps his hands together, and the light goes up. "Let's get these contracts taken care of."

CHAPTER 4

BRIAR

*I*t happens so fast.

Five separate voices snapping colors that correspond with the dresses we're wearing. I barely have time to process the silky, light voice that says, "Red," first, and then it's done. I know I heard someone say white, but the static in my brain ensures I couldn't describe the voice even with a gun to my head.

In the end, it doesn't matter.

The lights come up, and I get my first look at the small group gathered to claim us. I thought Azazel monstrous with his crimson skin and massive horns. He's nothing compared to the others gathered.

A rocky-looking creature with huge wings tucked back against his body. An obscenely tall, willowy woman who seems to be made of smoke and flames. A...I don't even know what to call him because I can barely focus on anything but the *tentacles*.

And an honest-to-god dragon man.

My false calm ripples, and a hysterical giggle bubbles up my throat. I swallow hard, determined to keep it down. I agreed to this. I might not have understood exactly what I was agreeing to, but I was not forced, and Azazel has given his word that it will continue to hold true.

No matter how monstrous they are, can they really be worse than Ethan?

Thinking about him is a mistake; the memories of right before I passed out come rushing back, of blood on Azazel's hands. My knees start to give out.

The woman in blue catches me under my elbow. "Steady," she murmurs. She doesn't sound any steadier than I feel, but I don't have the strength to point it out. Nor the cruelty.

We've made our beds. Now it's time to climb into them. With monsters.

I press my hand to my mouth as the giggle slides a few inches higher. Gods, I cannot lose control. Not now. Not here. Not ever.

Strange that I went from finding Azazel's crimson form horrifying to comforting in such a short time, but as he strides up to the dais, part of me honestly hopes he's about to tell us that the whole thing has been called off.

I'm a fool.

He casts a glance over our group. "There's a secondary contract to be signed, and then you'll be released into the custody of the one who claimed you." He focuses on me. "You first, Briar."

The woman in blue's grip tightens on my elbow as if she'll step between us, but what good will it do? I've agreed to this, and willingly. Changing my mind now is foolish and dangerous. I know what happens when someone with even a little bit of power gets told no. How much more does that hold true for demons and monsters?

"It's fine." My voice sounds perfectly normal as I carefully disengage from the woman in blue and take Azazel's outstretched hand. The dais is only a foot or so off the ground, but the little tremors working their way through my body suggest my legs might give out at any moment.

Again, time seems to move strangely. It must be shock, because I'm nearly certain there's no magic involved. I hadn't noticed the six doors ringing the room. One, we came in through, but I blink, and all five of us are standing in front of different doors. Another blink, and I'm stepping through mine and into a surprisingly lovely room with bookshelves, a thick rug covering most of the floor, and a comfortable looking couch that seems designed for hours spent reading. Not that I'd know. Ethan wasn't a fan of "lazy" activities, and reading was included on that list.

Azazel appears a few moments later, but it's the hulking form behind him that catches and holds my gaze. All the monsters were huge, but this one... The dragon. He's easily half a foot taller than Azazel, which means I'll barely come up to his chest if—when—we stand next to each other.

He's a strange mix of lizard and almost human, his head and face clearly leaning dragon, but his chest and arms looking more humanoid. Green scales cover the parts of his body I can see, ranging from a deep mossy color to one so pale, it's nearly white. Two short horn-looking things spear back from his temples that look to be a good six inches long. He's terrifying and strangely majestic, and he looks like he could break me in half without even trying.

"Let's begin."

I turn around and blink. A massive desk has appeared from nowhere. I didn't even feel a change in the air to indicate something had happened. *Why would the air change, Briar? The rules you've used to survive the old world won't apply in this one.* That horrible, hysterical giggle once again threatens to slip free. I press both my hands to my mouth and try to focus on breathing evenly and slowly.

Azazel sinks into a chair that *definitely* wasn't there a moment before. "Please sit."

A chair presses against the back of my thighs, and I jump, but my knees choose that moment to give up the ghost. I land on the seat with a thump that makes my bones rattle. I don't know if I'm supposed to say something, but I can't speak past the lump in my throat.

The dragon perches on a backless stool that has a half-moon carved out to accommodate his tail. I belatedly realize he's wearing pants, and I don't know why *that* detail nearly does me in, but I have to jerk my gaze to Azazel to keep from laughing. Or sobbing. At this point, it could go either way.

"This agreement will be slightly more unconventional than the others." Azazel's looking at me like I'm supposed to know what that means. "As promised in the original contract, you will not be coerced or forced, but you will allow Sol the opportunity to seduce you."

Seduced by a dragon. Sure. Why not?

The demon seems to be waiting for a response, so I give a jerky nod.

"However, dragon culture is a bit more..." He shoots a dark look at the dragon—at Sol. "Stringent. With that in mind, you'll be married for the duration of your time in our realm to avoid any unnecessary messiness."

"*What?*" It takes both of them staring at me to realize that squeaking word came from *me*. It should be enough to scare me into silence, but my brain has clicked offline. "I can't marry him. I'm already married."

"Ah." Azazel examines his black-clawed fingertips. "Technically, you're a widow."

Because he killed Ethan.

"Then I never want to get married again." It might be the dream we're sold as children, to end up standing before the altar with someone who loves you above all others and will be a partner against anything life throws at you, but that hasn't been my experience at all. Marriage is a bear trap closing around your leg, and the best you can do is cut off the appendage to get free and hope you don't bleed to death in the aftermath.

Having Ethan as a husband nearly killed me. How much worse will it be being married to a literal monster?

As if divining the direction of my thoughts, Azazel cuts in, "Similar to the contract that you signed with me, this contract will ensure the prescribed behavior on both parties' behalf. You won't be harmed."

I laugh bitterly. "Sure." There's no choice, though. Maybe there never was. Before I can talk myself out of it, I scoot forward, grab the pen next to the contract, and sign at the line above my name.

"Azazel—" It's the first time Sol has spoken since entering the room. I thought his voice would be sibilate, but I suppose dragons and snakes are hardly the same thing. Even so, I don't expect how deep the word is. He actually reaches out to grab my wrist but stops before making contact.

I stare at his hand; he could close it around my entire upper arm. My *thigh*. Maybe even my waist.

He's going to break me.

Sol makes a low hissing noise. "You never said she has a history of damage."

Damage. That's one way to put it. It might even be the truth.

"I'm a bargainer demon, dragon. Healthy, well-adjusted humans don't make bargains with demons. You chose. Deal with it."

The dragon hesitates for a long moment, clearly debating internally, before he takes the pen. It looks absurd in his scaled hand, but the size difference doesn't stop him from signing with a flourish. The sizzling feeling from last time surges through me and then disappears before I have a chance to tense. "Payment will be transferred over as soon as I return to the keep."

"Perfect." Azazel flicks a glance at me. "Keep in mind the stakes."

I blink. "You're speaking English."

Azazel is the one who answers. "There's a translation spell in effect for you. Anything spoken in your presence will be automatically translated in your mind."

Sol makes another of those hissing sounds. "Why doesn't she know about the spell, Azazel?"

"She was unconscious upon arriving. It was taken care of along with…" He stops short. "It hardly matters. It's done."

The dragon looks at me. "It's inked on your body, but the spell is linked deeper. It cannot be removed, even if the skin is."

"Are you planning on skinning me?" Once again, I blurt out the words without thinking.

"He's not." Azazel stands slowly. "If you harm so much as a hair on her head, your territory will be forfeit. The magic binding in the contract will know."

His territory.

I slump back against my chair. Well, fuck, I suppose that's a big enough stick to ensure good behavior, even from monsters. For the first time, it strikes me that Azazel has his own reasons for arranging this auction. Surely he has enough money that he doesn't need payment, no matter how much he's charging these monsters for us. If *territories* are on the line, that sounds a whole lot like a different word for *kingdom* or *country*. Either the demon really intends to keep us from harm…or he intends to ensure he takes every territory he can in payment.

If I were a betting woman, I would bet on the latter.

Azazel picks up the contract, and it vanishes in a surge of

shadows in his palm. "Ramanu will be along periodically to check on Briar. If you need anything, ask them and they will provide it." He glances at me. "Seven years and then you're free."

I was married to Ethan for thirteen. Surely I can survive this dragon for half that. A small price to pay for freedom. Or that's what I tell myself as I fight to my feet and follow the dragon out the door behind Azazel that I'm *certain* wasn't there before.

Sol opens it and steps back, motioning for me to precede him through. Instinct demands I don't leave him at my back, but what does it matter? He's a predator, from his size to his claws to the teeth he's flashed that are obviously meant for ripping and tearing prey. Having him behind me simply means I won't see my death coming.

I find that thought strangely comforting, which worries me a little bit. I take a breath and step through the doorway... into another world entirely.

CHAPTER 5

BRIAR

he first thing I notice is how different the air feels. It's as if I just stepped from a desert to the high mountains. I inhale deeply. Maybe not the high mountains. It just feels like the country, or at least how I imagine the country would smell. I've never spent much time outside the city. But it smells...green. I don't register Sol following me until the door shuts softly behind him.

It's right around that moment when I realize we're alone.

It leads into a wide and airy stone hallway. The blocks beneath my feet are so large, it defies comprehension that someone created a building with them, but the scale of everything seems larger in this...realm. There are even charming open arches overlooking greenery down below.

Even as I tell myself to hold still—that's what you're supposed to do with a predator, right?—I can't stop from scrambling away from Sol. The hallway that seemed to have plenty of space before is now too narrow with his presence filling it.

Sol looks down at me, his features too dragon for me to

read whatever emotion might be found there. "Come along." He moves down the hallway, leaving me to either follow or stay huddled here against the wall.

I try to calm my racing heart. He didn't do anything. He barely looked at me. Staying here might satisfy the terrified gibbering part of my brain, but if I'm to be here for seven years, I'm hardly going to spend it all in this hall.

It still takes far more bravery than I want to admit for me to push away from the wall and edge my way after Sol.

I move slowly to the half wall—which hits me about chest level—and peer down into a lush garden. Or I assume it's a garden. It looks like a mini forest, the only indication it's enclosed at all are the corners where my hallway makes a ninety-degree turn at either end.

"It's beautiful."

"You're welcome to explore. Later."

I jump nearly out of my skin. I'd been so enraptured by the garden I hadn't thought to clock Sol's location. I spin around to find him a few short feet away. Distantly, I'm aware enough to realize he's being very careful with me the same way I would be with a wild animal that wandered into my apartment. Not that there are many large wild animals in New York, but there are a lot of pigeons, and they can be real bastards.

I slap a hand to my mouth to keep my giggle inside. Not yet. I can lose my mind later. Right now, I have to focus. It takes several beats before I have enough control to drop my hand and say, "Okay."

Once again, he leads the way. I study his back as I follow him around the corner and through another series of halls leading away from the garden. His pants are obviously tailored around the existence of his tail. It's a nice enough tail, I guess. I don't know how such things are measured.

I've never seen a dragon before.

Now I'm about to be married to one.

Sol takes me down a set of stairs. I struggle with them, the height of the individual stairs different than I'm used to. Once we reach the ground floor, we start seeing other dragon people.

I'm too shell-shocked to remember not to stare, but it's just as well because they're staring at me, too. Some of them have breasts, which surprises me, though I don't know *why* it surprises me. Sol is obviously a dragon *person*, rather than just a dragon. He has pecs, for fuck's sake.

Moving helps keep my panic at bay. I can't quite make the details of the place and its people stick in my head. The only thing I truly register is that the dragon people seem to be a wide variety of shades of either brown or green.

Another door leads us outside to a heavily wooded area with a neatly maintained gravel path. There, Sol slows until he's walking next to me. "The ceremony won't be long, and then you can rest."

I miss a step. No matter how I cling to the calm, it's slipping through my fingers. "I don't want to be married again." I agreed to it. I signed the damn contract. It doesn't mean it's what I want, though. I should be going along with this, making him happy, but I can't quite manage it.

"It's necessary."

I have every intention of keeping my mouth shut, but this has been too much in too short a time. "In case I have a kid."

"Yes."

Later, I'll appreciate that he's not trying to talk circles around me and make me doubt myself. Maybe. I lift my chin, staring up into his dark eyes. If he opened his mouth, he could probably bite my head clean off. "How would that even work? You're massive and I'm human. Having a kid would kill me."

"The magic mixes in a way that prevents that." He's holding still, answering me patiently even as the answers make me want to flee. "To my understanding, children are born humanoid in size and features and then become more dragon-like as they grow in the first year or so."

"To your understanding," I repeat. "You don't know."

"There hasn't been a human-dragon child in generations. It's why you're here."

I stop suddenly. "Azazel says you can't force me."

He rears back, his crest flaring a deep orange flash that startles me. Sol makes that hissing noise. "No one is going to *force* you to do anything. I don't know what it's like in the human realm, but we're civilized here."

The giggle I've been fighting to contain bursts free. "Civilized. Right." I wrap my arms around myself and bend in half, gasping for breath. "As if there's a society in existence that doesn't have sins. Please."

The bones go out of my legs, and I start to slump to the ground. Sol moves faster than he has a right to, scooping me up and continuing down the path as if nothing happened. I try to tense up, to demand he put me down, but my body and brain won't cooperate.

Instead, I slump against his broad chest and let him carry me, his long strides eating up the distance and taking us away from the building. His body is so warm, his scales curiously soft against my cheek. No, soft isn't the right word. Maybe smooth? He's almost pebbly in a really pleasing way that makes me want to drag my fingers over him.

That thought brings me back to myself.

I will *not* be touching this dragon man in any way that might be construed as an invitation. I open my mouth to tell him to put me down, but the path opens up, the trees falling away to reveal a clearing tucked back against a low cliff face. A small waterfall trickles down into a pond about the size of a very large hot tub. The soft sound of water instantly loosens something in my chest. Or maybe it's the golden light that filters through the trees overhead. Something about the space feels like I just popped one of my fast-acting anxiety meds. "What is this place?"

"The sacred grove associated with this part of our territory. There are four in the dragon lands, and the location of the keep was chosen for its proximity to this spring." He carefully sets me down, his big hands spanning my waist and then some. "All our rituals and important events happen here."

I turn in a slow circle. The clearing is larger than I first thought; the sheer size of the trees make it feel more closed in than it should be. Still, if there are only four locations in... dragon lands... "Are they all this size?"

He follows my gaze. "No. This is the smallest of the four. It's meant only for those in the keep and my family."

I'll have more questions later. The curiosity that gave me a boost of energy is already fading. "Oh."

"Come." He moves to the edge of the spring, and I follow a few steps behind. This close, I can see the water is perfectly clear and there are natural steps leading down. Sol motions at them. "We enter separately and emerge as one."

"*This* is your marriage ceremony?"

It's hard to tell, but I think he's biting back a hiss of frustration. "Yes."

I frown at the spring, waiting for my earlier panic to surge forth. This isn't anything like my last wedding. There's no crowd of friends and family. No carefully curated color scheme. No walking down an aisle to a man I thought was my Prince Charming.

Honestly, it sounds more like a baptism than anything else, but I've never been overly religious, so that's one of the few things about this scenario I don't find triggering.

I can do this.

I nod slowly. "Okay." He starts to move, but I throw up a hand. "Can I go first?" Descending to him might not be close to last time, but I'd rather not risk it.

Sol motions with his clawed and scaled hand. "By all means."

It's not until I'm carefully navigating down the steps that I realize the dress is going to be a problem. The layers of fabric go sheer as they hit the water.

Oh well. We're about to be married and he wants to seduce me into having his children. I'm too tired to care about a little nudity. "This doesn't mean anything."

"It does to me." He hesitates. "But no, this isn't an invitation for anything but the marriage itself."

There's no use arguing. His compromise, if it can be called that, is enough to reassure me. I take a deep breath and finish descending into the spring.

The water is warm and comes to my chest. I don't know why that surprises me. Nothing about this situation has been what I expected, so why should this? I trail my fingers through the water and turn to find Sol watching me.

His expression is too alien for me to read. I think I detect hunger, but is it sexual or violent? He hasn't done anything to harm me, but we've been alone for a less than an hour. Surely he's too smart to break his contract with Azazel so quickly? It took Ethan months before he started encroaching on my confidence, whittling away at *me*. That old saying about the frog in boiling water has more than a little truth to it. We'd been married three years before he hurt me physically the first time.

Sol moves, jerking my attention back to the present. He descends the steps smoothly, and I can't help examining his body. His chest is very human, broad shoulders descending to well-defined pecs and a solid stomach. I *should* stop looking there, but curiosity sinks its claws in deep and drags my gaze farther south to where the water licks at his hips, molding his pants to his body. The intent way he watches me sharpens, and the front of his pants shifts.

Look away.

Stop staring.

I don't. I stand there, frozen, and watch his cock harden just from the sight of me, from my attention on him. Except it looks strange and... I blink. "You have *two* cocks."

"Yes."

My mouth works, but I can't find words. *Two.* And they look to be in proportion with him, which means they're massive. I don't... What... "*Two.*"

"Briar."

His saying my name for the first time is enough to pull my gaze from his hips and up to his face. Sol makes a hissing sound that seems almost agonized. "You're not making an offer to do more than look."

It's not a question. I have no reason to argue. He's talking like he fully intends to honor Azazel's promises, which boggles my mind. The curiosity coursing through me only gets stronger, but I wrestle it back under control. "Have you been with humans before? Are you even sure it will fit?"

"It will fit," he grinds out.

So he *has* been with humans before. I frown but understanding dawns quickly. "Azazel really is clever, isn't he? He gave you a taste before this with others."

"Yes, but this bargain isn't about sex." He stalks past me, keeping a careful distance between us. "Now, stop talking about my cock unless you intend to do something about it."

I snap my mouth shut against a horrifyingly flirty response. This man—this dragon—might be strangely intriguing, but that doesn't mean I'm about to do more than look. Even if I were...

No.

The consequences are too dire. It's not worth it for simple curiosity.

CHAPTER 6

SOL

I don't fancy myself particularly unrestrained, but this strange little human woman is testing my limits already. She stands here in one of our holiest of holy springs, her white dress transparent as the water licks at her pink nipples and has the audacity to stare at my cocks with something resembling desire.

It was easier with the other humans. They came to me with their intention already negotiated—bargainer demons treat a good negotiation almost like foreplay, I swear. There was no need for careful circling of each other. I enjoyed my time with them and went on my way afterward.

This is different.

Briar isn't a human looking for some fun for a night. In a few moments, she'll be my wife. More, even in the short time we've spent alone, I can't deny there's something startlingly fragile about her. As if by moving too quickly, I might bruise her.

I stop short of the waterfall and hold out my hand. I've been too abrupt with her, but there's no point in taking the words back. They're true, after all.

To her credit, she doesn't flee. I don't know what I'd do if she did. Chase her, yes. But only because I can't have a terrified human wandering my lands. There are predators far scarier than me in the woods surrounding the keep, let alone farther afield.

The rationalization feels like a lie. I am not a beast, but I desire this woman, and sometimes instincts go a little funny. Especially after a marriage ceremony. Even now, my people are mostly clearing out of the keep. Only those essential to the running of this territory will remain. Marriages of convenience aren't customary with my people, and none of us are quite sure what will happen after this ceremony. Normally, a careful courtship evolves into a marriage if both parties are happy with the relationship. I've only entered into one courting relationship, and my parents put a stop to things with Anika before we were able to decide for ourselves if it was something we wanted to make permanent. For their part, Anika didn't seem particular broken up to have the courtship cut off, though we're still friends.

If I were anyone else, even a younger child, I could marry for love. But my happiness is not worth sacrificing the health of an entire territory for. The last leader of the bargainer demons kept the borders closed and her resources fiercely guarded. Azazel took over sometime after I was born, and by the time I reached maturity, my parents made it clear that I needed to seek out a human bride if at all possible.

No matter what I personally wanted.

This relationship, if it can be called that, isn't mirroring a normal one. I have no idea if the mating frenzy will be a factor at all the same way it would be with another dragon. We're all playing cautious, though. Just in case.

Even so...

"Don't run from me."

She pauses in the middle of reaching for my hand, her

brows winging up. Reading human body language is not natural to me despite the time I've spent in their company. Dragons are simpler. I know instantly if another dragon is approaching in threat, though we don't engage in the dominance plays some of the other types of demons do. We're civilized.

When Briar speaks, there's a strange thread in her voice that I can't quantify. "What will you do if I run?"

The truth likely isn't the answer she wants, but I don't lie. Even when it would serve me. "I'll chase you." I do *not* allow myself to picture what that would be like. The only path forward between us is a careful dance as I win her over. Nowhere in that exchange does it include chasing her down and ripping her clothing off with my teeth. She's already terrified out of her mind. I clamp down on every instinct I have to ensure I don't make it worse.

"I see." She places her hand in mine. "I won't run unless I want you to chase me."

There's nothing I can say that will be even remotely appropriate, so I turn us toward the waterfall. "The waters here are our goddess's tears."

"Tears at a wedding. How apt," she murmurs, almost too low to be heard over the water.

"Tears are transformative. They aren't only for sad times."

"I wouldn't know." This time, I'm certain she didn't intend for me to hear that.

Something strange and almost protective stirs to life inside me. The humans I've interacted with to date seem happy with their bargainer contracts and live a life free from worry about anything but giving and receiving pleasure. Not all of them engage in sexual activities, of course. But on the rare invitations to Azazel's castle, he very intentionally opens the doors to those who are happy and willing to play.

Briar is different. I didn't notice it during the auction, but she carries herself as if she's wounded, though I can scent no injury on her. If I thought he'd answer truly, I'd ask Azazel what the price of her contract was. I have a feeling it would be illuminating.

"We entered separately." I tug Briar beneath the waterfall. The cascade instantly soaks her red hair, plastering it to her neck and shoulders, and she has to grab for her dress to keep it in place. I almost tell her there's no point—the fabric has long since gone sheer—but if it makes her feel better, then I won't be the one to ruin that.

We stand there for three beats. She's right that normally there is more ceremony for a ritual like this, but ultimately the only thing required is two—or more—willing parties and the spring itself. Everything else is extra.

We emerge from the waterfall together, and I attempt not to look into the fact she doesn't immediately drop my hand. "We leave as one."

Walking up the stairs next to her feels strange. Even as I command myself to look away, I can't help studying the body revealed by the now-sheer dress. She's tinier than I expected, and despite my earlier assurances, I wonder if I *will* fit. Maybe others' tastes run to pain, but that's never been my preferred flavor of pleasure. I suspect the same is true for this woman.

Getting ahead of yourself.

Without thinking, I sweep her into my arms. This time, she doesn't tense. She simply melts against me in a way that makes my chest feel strange. It's not trust; we don't know each other well enough to justify something as foundational as trust. But it's something.

The few of my people left in the keep make themselves scarce as I carry Briar through the doors and up the stairs to the rooms that were supposed to be ours. Hopefully they will be in the future, but even if the woman doesn't look at me with fear and revulsion, she's hardly ready for any kind of bed sport. Even now, tiny tremors work through her body, and I can't begin to tell if it's because her wet dress is causing her to be chilled or if it's a renewed fear.

Still, it takes more control than I'll ever admit to set her carefully on her feet in front of the bedroom door. "You'll find everything you need through here. I'll have supper sent up shortly." I pause, belated concern flaring. "Do you have dietary restrictions?"

She stares up at me, her eyes slightly glazed. "Are you going to serve me raw meat or something poisonous?"

"I wasn't planning on it." Or at least I'm not now. I don't know *what* is poisonous to humans. Obviously there is food in our realm humans can eat, or the bargainers wouldn't be able to have humans staying on in a long-term contract, but while my people might have common ancestors with Briar's people, that doesn't change the fact we are obviously different in a number of biological ways.

"Then no. No dietary restrictions."

I'll ensure that before having food sent up. "Good. Rest."

She opens the door but doesn't step through. "Sol."

Goddess, but it affects me to hear my name on her lips. I hold perfectly still. "Yes?"

"In the contract, it says you can seduce me…"

I have to lock down every muscle to keep from doing something to spook her. I may not be an expert on humans, but even I can tell she's not entirely sure what she wants my answer to be. *That's better than pure fear. I can work with that.* "Rest, Briar. I'll see you in the morning."

I force myself to turn and move away from her, though my senses are keen enough that I know she doesn't enter the bedroom until I've rounded the corner of the hall. Watching me leave? Or ensuring that I don't follow her into the bedroom?

It doesn't matter. I can be a patient hunter.

The prize is more than worth a little discomfort in the meantime.

CHAPTER 7

BRIAR

*I*t takes more courage than I'll ever admit to strip
down and utilize the gargantuan bathtub to warm
up after the trip back from the spring. No one appears to
take advantage of my nakedness, though, and I almost fall
asleep cradled in the scalding warmth of the water.

At least until I hear someone moving about in the
bedroom. I jerk up, fear thick in my throat. "Who's there?"

"Aldis." A brown dragon peeks her head into the bathroom. "I brought up human-approved food and got a fire
going. It gets chilly at night this time of year."

I sink deeper into the water. I'm not sure how I feel about
the fact that this isn't Sol. "Oh. Thank you."

She studies me for a long moment. "It's a lot to take in.
Don't worry. Sol's a grump, but he'll be good to you."

I'm not touching *that* with a ten-foot pole. "If you say so."

"Also, here's a robe." She ducks into the bathroom and
drapes a long length of fabric over the hook near the sink.
"We dragons are a bit larger than you, but it should work
until we get some clothing tailored."

It's all too much. My brain feels fuzzy and slow. "Thank you," I manage.

It's hard to tell, but Aldis gives me what seems to be a kind expression. "We have some adjustments ahead of us. Please try to give Sol a bit of grace, and I'm sure he'll do the same for you." She's gone before I can come up with a response to that.

It's just as well. I'm exhausted and fresh out of grace.

* * *

SOL DOESN'T COME to see me the next morning. Or the one after that. By the third day, I tell myself I'm relieved and not disappointed. Yes, that must be the source of the sinking sensation in my stomach. *Relief*.

Or maybe it's boredom.

I'm nearly certain the rooms he gave me are actually his. It's more than the large bed situated low on the floor, the mattress made of some material I don't recognize. No, the thing that makes me certain these rooms are Sol's are the little mementos tucked about.

The high table is scattered with books and papers written in a language I don't understand. There are more books stacked haphazardly on shelves about the room, enough that I can't help thinking about the old legends in my world about dragons and their hoards. I bet he has a proper library somewhere in this place. Not that it will do me any good. Apparently my new tattoo—a strange symbol inked in a deep red on my right shoulder blade—doesn't extend its translation magic to the written word.

There is clothing as well, all Sol-sized and tailored for someone with, well, a tail. On the second day, Aldis returns to deliver a chest full of human clothing. She doesn't linger

45

this time, though. She ducks out of the room so fast, I'm still deciding if I want to try to strike up a conversation. I'm not sure where they got the clothing, but it fits perfectly.

On the third day, I tell myself I'm only wearing in the white dress with its empire waist and low neckline because it's comfortable and makes me feel pretty. *Not* because of the way Sol stared at my breasts in the spring.

A knock on the door has my heartbeat picking up. In *fear*, not excitement. Surely. I cross my arms and say, "Come in."

The person who walks through the door is not Sol. They're not even a dragon. I stare at the crimson skin and the horns sprouting from their eye socket. A second set curls back from their temples. "Who are you, and what are you doing in my room?"

"Ramanu." They press a black-clawed hand to their wide chest. They're dressed much the same as Azazel was during the auction—black pants and a black tunic-type shirt that's belted about the waist, all made of obviously expensive materials. "Azazel sent me to…take stock of the situation."

They appear to be looking around the room, and I barely manage to stop from blurting out a question asking *how* when they don't have eyes. Obviously some magic is involved. Still, I don't like the mocking little smile pulling at the edges of their almost-human mouth. I draw myself up. "There's no situation to take stock of."

"Hmmm." They step into the room and utter a soft laugh when I tense further. "You have nothing to fear from me. Even if Azazel wouldn't skin me alive for touching one of his precious contracted humans, I like my playmates with a bit more…" Their smile turns into a full grin. "Spice."

I don't know if they mean that figuratively or literally, and I'm not about to ask. If *this* is who Azazel is sending to check up on people… I shudder. "As I said, there's no situation to take stock of."

"Now, that's interesting." They meander about the room, taking up too much space. They're shorter than Sol by a good six inches even with the horns, but I keep expecting their horns to scrape on the ceiling. "Fascinating that the blessed dragon leader has already managed to scare off his human bride."

I just met this demon, and I barely know Sol at all, but that doesn't stop me from firing back, "He's a gentleman. He hasn't done a single thing wrong." I don't know why I'm defending him. Maybe he eats puppies in his free time. Do they even have puppies in this realm?

"A gentleman." They laugh. "He is, that." They move to the door and cast a look over their shoulder. Or at least I think they do. "Come along, little bride. Let's find your wayward dragon husband."

Nothing good can come of this. Obviously Ramanu wants to stir the pot; they haven't exactly been a sympathetic ear in the short time they've been in my presence, and, beyond that, there is obviously tension between Azazel and the other leaders.

Still, I'm curious, and I've been cooped up for days. Sol never came to see me. Wandering the keep with a demon at my side isn't exactly peaceful, but surely it's better than wandering about alone?

I'm hurrying after Ramanu before I can think of a good reason not to. They stride through the halls with an easy confidence, and I honestly can't tell if they're faking it or if they know where they're going. They did find my room, though. Maybe they've been here before.

We go down a set of stairs and through a series of halls that look out into the garden. Again, I'm tempted to stop and stare and soak up the atmosphere that comes from the trees and flowers. Sol's bedroom has an interior window overlooking the private park—I'm not sure what else to call it, because *garden* doesn't feel like it encompasses the feeling—which is the only reason I've lasted in the room as long as I have.

It's been...peaceful. But too much peace has boredom closing in.

Ramanu's long strides have me half skipping to keep up. I'm about to snap at them to slow down when they stop in front of a door that looks just like every other one we've passed up to this point. They give me another of those unsettling grins, and then they throw open the door.

I make it one step through the door and stop short. A *library*. It stretches up two floors, lined with more books than I can comprehend, the walls curving backward into shadows, giving the impression of a truly massive room.

A dragon hoard.

While I'm staring in awe, Ramanu has tossed their large body into an overstuffed chair, one of half a dozen varied pieces of furniture arranged in a cozy little sitting area off to the side of the door. I wander closer to them, still trying to take in the sheer size of the room.

They tilt back their head and bellow, "I know you're in here, dragon. Come out, come out, wherever you are."

"Goddess damn it, Ramanu. Who let you in here?" Sol steps out from between two stacks and stops short. "Briar."

"Someone's been neglecting their pretty little bride." They reach over and catch the hem of my dress where it brushes just below my knee. I don't miss the fact that they don't actually touch my skin, but I can only guess what it must look like from where Sol's standing.

A dangerous hissing sound fills the room. "Take your hand off her."

"You're not touching her. Why shouldn't I?"

I don't know why Ramanu is baiting Sol, but I don't like it. I step back and swat at their hand. "That's enough."

They turn that strange horned face in my direction. "You really are perfect for each other. Neither one of you has a sense of humor." They glance back at Sol. "If she dies from neglect, that's still harm."

The dragon huffs out a breath. His crest flares, and the hissing sound deepens. "Get out."

Ramanu chuckles as they stand. "All this effort, all this risk, and you're mishandling the situation. I can't pretend I'm even a little surprised." They meander toward the door. "I'll be around at some point to check on her. Maybe you'll have stopped being a coward by then."

Then they're gone, leaving a growing awkward silence in their wake.

The temptation to flee the room is strong, but I remember Sol's words from when he took me to the spring. *If you run, I'll chase you.* That possibility should fill me with fear, and I won't pretend there's not a thread of it present. But it's not the dominant emotion. I don't know what's wrong with me. I'd promised myself that if—*when*—I escaped my marriage, I would be cautious and careful and do whatever it took to never repeat history.

Now, here I stand, wondering what it would be like for Sol to chase me, to pounce on me, to...

I shake my head. "I'm sorry. I didn't realize they intended to bait you, or I wouldn't have come with them."

"Ramanu is one of Azazel's most challenging people." Sol snorts, and I imagine I can feel the hot air of it despite the distance between us. He hefts the book in his hand and starts moving toward me in a way that's almost reluctant. "I think that's why he delights in sending them here any chance he gets."

"Why did you do it?" This time, I manage not to clap my hands over my mouth after I blurt out the question, but it's a near thing. "You took a great risk bargaining with him. What if I fall down the stairs and snap my neck?"

His crest flares again, though his voice is even. "Would you like me to move you to the ground floor?"

"What? No. That's not what I mean, and you know it." I lift my hands and let them drop to my sides. Why would he confide in me? He doesn't know me at all. "I just want to understand."

Sol sinks onto a deep chair and curls his tail around to make room. I stare. I hadn't realized it was prehensile. There is absolutely no reason for that knowledge to send a surge of heat through my body. What is *wrong* with me?

For his part, he doesn't seem to notice how he's affecting me. He leans back and drops the book on the cushion next to him. "There was a time when the realms—mortal, demon, divine—were closer together. Or easier to cross." He looks away, dark eyes going thoughtful. "There are a lot of theories why that changed, and no one quite knows for sure what happened. Obviously humans used to be here in greater numbers." He motions to himself, to his humanoid body.

That makes sense in a strange sort of way. There are tales across many cultures about people stepping into fairy circles or answering strange voices calling in the night and never being seen again. It's not so hard to believe they crossed into a different realm, especially considering where I'm standing right now.

But knowing that still doesn't explain why Sol risked his entire kingdom for a human bride. Especially when he's obviously avoiding said bride.

"Did Ramanu frighten you?" He studies me intently. "I won't pretend they're harmless, because they're more assuredly *not*, but Azazel's contracts are good. Ramanu won't hurt you."

Honestly, after I got over the eye horns, Ramanu is more

infuriating than anything else, but I find myself nodding. "Yes, they frightened me." *What are you doing?* I ignore the very reasonable voice in my head and press forward. "Would you… Could…" I drag in a breath. "Could I sit with you until I calm down?"

CHAPTER 8

BRIAR

*I*t's blatantly clear Sol had every intention of sending me back to my room. It's equally clear that I've shocked him with the request to sit with him. That's fair. I've shocked myself. My damned curiosity has a hold of me, and the fact Sol is obviously trying his best not to overwhelm or scare me is...

I don't know.

I hardly feel like myself as he nods slowly and lifts a hand in obvious invitation. It's not until I'm moving, carefully placing my hand in his, that my brain catches up enough to ask me *where* I intend to sit.

In that moment, if Sol pulled me onto his lap, I honestly don't know what I'd do.

He doesn't. Of course he doesn't. He simply tugs me to sit at his side. His tail shifts against my back, tightening the slightest amount, scooting me closer until we're plastered together from knee to shoulder. He's so *warm*. I don't even think to tense. I melt instead.

Sol awkwardly drapes his massive arm around my shoulders, and the sheer size of him has my lower stomach doing strange things. By all rights, I should be terrified of him. Ethan taught me many hard lessons over the course of our marriage, the first being that my instincts are trash. I trusted that man enough to marry him and look what happened.

With my track record, Sol is more likely to eat me whole than to be kind to me, contract or no.

Maybe that's the difference. The contract. The stakes are so high—so much higher for him than they are for me—that I feel safe. That must be it. It's the only logical explanation. I relax against him further. The texture of his scales against my cheek really is nice. He's smooth and warm and...

"How would it work?"

Sol goes so still against me, he might as well have turned to stone. "Excuse me?"

"Sex. That's why you were there at the auction, right? Or you were there for a bride to have children with, but children are often a product of sex, so the question stands. How would it work?" Though I don't know if it was actually an auction in the strictest sense of the word. As far as I can tell, there was no bidding or funds exchanged. They just claimed each one of us and then signed a contract with their territories in the balance. At least if the terms of the other contracts were the same as Sol's and mine.

He still hasn't moved. "We don't need to talk about this."

"I kind of think we do." It's easier without looking at him, trying to read his expression when I'm still not familiar enough to pull it off. Body language is simpler. He hisses and flares his crest when agitated, and neither of those things are happening right now. What's more, he's still keeping his touch on me carefully light as if he's afraid I'll bolt if he moves too quickly.

Or as if he's deciding whether *he* wants to bolt right now.

"Though, if you intend to seduce me, you're going about it strangely. Or is this one of those hunting games predators play? I don't have much to go on, and I'd like not to make assumptions because there are obvious cultural differences between us."

He shudders out a very human-sounding breath. "You didn't want to be married."

Of all the things I anticipated him saying, this didn't number among them. I blink. "What does that have to do with anything?"

"You were married before." His tail shifts against my back, tucking me closer yet. "That's why you made your bargain with Azazel."

I don't particularly want to talk about my past, but it's hard to cling to that when I'm so far beyond Ethan's reach. If the blood on Azazel's hands was any indication, I'm out of his reach forever.

I won't shed my fear so easily, won't stop looking over my shoulder when I finally return to my realm. Being here? Like this? It almost feels like a dream. Like nothing bad can touch me.

Dangerous thoughts.

You're disassociating.

Maybe. Maybe it's pure self-preservation, but until Sol gives me a reason not to trust the demon contract, I can let this comfortable numbness twine with my curiosity for a little longer. "Yes," I finally say. "I do believe he intended to kill me before he let me go. My husband, I mean. Not Azazel, of course." My voice doesn't sound quite right.

A hiss rattles through Sol's chest. "You must think highly of me to expect me try seducing you when you're practically bleeding out at my feet."

I sit up. "I'm not bleeding. Azazel healed my wounds. Or had someone else do it."

He jolts, and I realize that was exactly the wrong thing to say. Sol looks down at me, and for the first time, I realize how warm his dark eyes normally are, because they're not right now. They're cold and dangerous, and I've never been more reminded that he is predator and I am prey than in this moment.

I do what all prey animals do when running means death. I freeze.

He holds me captive with that stare for several torturous beats of my racing heart. "You insult me."

Common sense says to shut the hell up, but my common sense has gone the way of my fear, smothered beneath numbness and curiosity and the tiniest spark of desire. He's angry at me, yes, but he's also angry on my behalf. It's strange. "Why wouldn't you want sex if I were offering? I thought all men want sex all the time?" That's certainly how Ethan acted.

His hisses louder. "Fine, Briar. Would you like to know how sex would work with us?" His tail loosens around me, taking its glorious warmth with it, and he slides his arm from my shoulders to the back of the couch. I'm adrift, which makes his next words hit like hammer blows. "I'm not interested in splitting you in half, so I'll rip off whatever charming little dress you're wearing with my teeth and then taste you until you're riding my tongue and begging for more. Then, if I'm feeling particularly generous, I'll give you both my cocks, one at a time."

"Wait," I whisper.

He leans down, his hot breath ruffling my hair. "And then I'm going to fill you up, Briar. How much of me can you take? There's only one way to find out."

My body takes off while my mind is still trying to process the full depth of his promise. I'm on my feet with no memory of making the decision to stand. "You are *such* an asshole." I flee the room, but not so quickly that I miss his low statement biting at my heels.

"If you're so determined to think me a monster, then I'll play monster for you."

It's not until I find my way back to my room, heart still beating too hard and breath coming too fast, that I realize what just happened. I ran. And he didn't chase me.

I slam the door, and I can't decide if I'm angrier at him or myself. I blundered that, and badly. I had to rely on *Sol* to slam us back into safe territory, because if he'd flirted a little and kept up that intoxicating warmth against my body, I might have forgotten all my determination to stay away from him and done something unforgivable.

It's the numbness's fault.

Or maybe my curiosity is to blame.

I drop onto the edge of the mattress and curse. It feels good to snarl words that would have gotten me into danger with Ethan, so I do it again. "That fucking *asshole*." I don't know if I'm talking about Sol or Ethan or maybe even myself. I stand and drag my hands through my hair.

I don't know what's *wrong* with me. I'm not acting like my usually careful, cautious self. There is nothing careful or cautious about dangling sex in front of Sol to see what he'd do. Because that's exactly what I was up to when I asked that question.

Well. I know what he'll do now.

Pacing about the room does little to bleed off the adrenaline surging through my system. That must be to blame for the images that take up residence just behind my eyes. Of Sol ripping through this dress with those sharp teeth, of him bearing me down to the ground and spreading my legs with rough, but careful, movements. His mouth is so big, he'd have to practically encase me to get his tongue to my pussy. I shiver at the bolt of pure lust that nearly takes me off my feet.

All those sharp teeth pressed against my vulnerable skin. His tongue on me...*in* me.

Once again, my body takes over, but this time my mind is fully on board with the idea. I drag off the dress and flop back onto the bed. There were no underthings in the clothing Aldis provided, so there's nothing in the way of my questing fingers as I slide my hand down my stomach and spread my legs.

I'm so wet. God, I can't believe how turned on I am.

And...*two cocks.*

I press two fingers into my pussy. Better to focus on the fantasy, because surely reality can't be as good as my mind insists. I didn't like any kind of sex with Ethan. There's no reason to believe it would be different with Sol. It's just pretend, though, and nothing can hurt in my mind.

The temptation to push through, to make this quick and furtive, nearly overwhelms me. I didn't masturbate often up to this point, because I was always aware that if I were caught, it wouldn't go well for me. That kind of thing puts a damper on pleasure, at least for me.

But if *Sol* caught me?

If he walked through the door right now and saw me with my hand between my legs? What would he do? Take it as an invitation? Or maybe he'd sit in that chair right there and watch.

He's so controlled. Even knowing him such a short time, I recognize that. I don't know if I'd have the courage to actually invite him to touch me, but this is just fantasy. In my mind, he comes to stand at the edge of the bed. To press one of those big knees to the mattress and lean over me. To...

I pick up my pace. My orgasm is too close to stop, too strong to do anything but ride out with a low moan that I don't even think to muffle. I whimper and jerk my fingers away from my clit. Now is when the shame will come, ruining the afterglow.

Except...it doesn't.

I stare at the ceiling as my racing heart finally slows and the languid pleasure of my orgasm makes my eyelids heavy. Maybe things are different here, after all. At least in this. I pull the blankets around me and roll over to settle into bed.

I can admit—if only to myself—that I wouldn't have minded so much if *that* fantasy had played out in reality.

CHAPTER 9

SOL

$\mathcal{I}$ brace my hands against the wall and press my forehead to the door. The steadiness of stone and wood ground me even as desire beats a drum through my blood. I can *scent* Briar's desire, her need. I flick my tongue into the air, tasting the way she's drenched the sheets with her orgasm. My hearing isn't as acute as some of the other species in this realm, but Briar's little whimper of release will be imprinted on my soul for the rest of my days.

I came to apologize. I was too harsh with her. She's coming out of a traumatic event and she doesn't know me. Instead of encouraging her fledgling curiosity, I *scared* her. More, she doesn't know this world, and she's been cut adrift from anything tethering her to her home realm.

Is it any wonder she's doing what it takes to survive? To ensure her safety?

But every word she spoke, how easily she dismissed her own pain and experiences... It grates on me. I can't claim to know her. The knowing of a person takes a lifetime, and even then, there will be depths left to plumb. A few short days of playing the coward and ignoring her had done little to bridge the gap between us.

Perhaps that's what she's attempting, in her own way.

I force myself to push back from the wall and walk away from the door. It's a good sign that I didn't traumatize her with my harsh words. Obviously her interest in sex isn't completely feigned, but there is her history to consider. Mainly, that I need to know it.

Azazel has that information. It irks me to go begging to him for scraps of details about Briar, but at this juncture, I need all the help I can get. Harm isn't only in the domain of the physical, and the demon is too savvy not to have taken that into account. I should have remembered than when I spoke so rashly in the library.

I could lose my territory because I let Briar's recklessness guide us. I don't wish to harm the woman.

Aldis is waiting for me as I descend the stairs. I eye her. "I have somewhere to be."

"You do, cousin. Several letters have come in for you, and they are of the utmost importance. Also, the paperwork you've been avoiding for days." Her eyes shine merrily. There is nothing my cousin loves more than paperwork; it's why I gave her the position of scribe to begin with. We dragons don't bother with a formal court. Most of us are territorial and have long memories, and it's easier to confine correspondence to the written word and let everyone stay in their own territories within our land.

We are creatures of tradition, and while that can drive me up the wall from time to time, it certainly does make being king easier. At least on this subject.

I hesitate, which is exactly what I need for reason to take hold. Azazel gives away nothing for free, and going to him with questions will ensure he knows how badly I'm bungling this. No, better to feel through the situation by instinct. Regardless of the regrets I have for speaking to Briar the way I did—no matter how truthful the words were—it's obvious I didn't harm her with them.

We can do this. We can figure this out. Together.

But first, apparently I have some paperwork to get through. I follow Aldis to the study and barely hold back a groan at the stacks of paper waiting for me. "Did something happen?"

"It's second harvest season." She shrugs.

Ah. Of course. If I hadn't been so preoccupied with Azazel's offer and what it might entail, this wouldn't have crept up on me. Each territory in this realm runs a little differently, and while there is some trade, all us leaders are loathe to rely on each other for fear that it will tip the power balance. Because of that, at some point in the distant past, one of my ancestors completely overhauled our internal industries. Only about half of our territory is farmland, but it's more than enough to feed our people. Twice a year, when various crops come to harvest, everything is gathered and redistributed to all. It allows us to share crops and make the most of the land available, while also ensuring that everyone has a bit of variety. If, for some reason, one crop fails during one of the harvests, no one will go hungry.

This task can't be put off.

I find myself glancing at the ceiling in the direction of my rooms. "Aldis, while I get started on this, can you put in an order with the kitchen for dinner?"

She goes still. "So you're finally going to stop ignoring your bride. Lovely."

"If I wanted your opinion, I'd ask for it."

"Sometimes you need opinions even if you don't ask for them." She props her hands on her hips. "You took a huge risk bringing her here and marrying her. I know your parents were the ones to call off the courtship with Anika, but there are plenty of our people who were very happy to have them as a leader at your side. Anika is familiar. This human isn't."

"Anika isn't the one stirring the pot." Why would they? About a year after my parents stepped in, they fell in love with a reclusive dragon who lives on the edge of our territory where it bumps up against the gargoyles' mountains. "They're too busy with their little one and husband to worry about what I'm doing." At that, I *do* feel a bit of a twinge.

I want children. I always have. I'm happy for Anika, but there's a tiny thread of envy in there. I want that happily contented life, too.

"No, it's not Anika. And it's only grumbling at this point. Nothing to worry about, but I still wanted you to be aware of it."

This is one of those leadership things that I don't enjoy. Taking care of my people? It brings me such joy and pride. Dealing with the petty squabbles or politicking? Not so much. Especially in this, when I'm following my late parents' wishes, Goddess hold them gently. "The entire territory stands to benefit from this marriage, and they know it. The only reason they're complaining at all is because complaining is a sport to them."

"True." Aldis motions to the desk. "Now stop stalling and get to work. I'll go down to the kitchen."

I sink into the chair behind the desk. "Tell them to cook whatever Briar's been eating."

"Mm-hmm." Aldis's amusement filters through her tone, but when I look up to hiss, she's already gone. It's just as well.

Earlier, Briar asked me why I hadn't attempted to seduce her. I had thought to give her time to settle in, but in this moment, I can admit the truth. I was acting the part of the coward just like Ramanu accused me of being. After this morning, the fact I didn't scare off my bride for good…

It's time to seduce her properly.

Starting tonight.

CHAPTER 10

BRIAR

I pace the room, my gown swishing around my bare feet. Dragons don't wear shoes, I've discovered, and even if they did, they wouldn't fit my feet. I have no reason to be nervous and certainly no reason to feel guilty. Except no matter how many times I tell myself that, I can't make it stick.

Earlier today, I was a bit of an ass. I could tell Sol was uncomfortable, and I pushed him despite that. Then, when he spilled those sinful words that he obviously meant to sound as a threat, I immediately went back to my room and touched myself to the fantasy of them.

By all rights, I should be terrified out of my mind, but it's not knives slicing at the inside of my stomach. It's...butterflies?

I spin to the mirror, mostly to give myself something to do. I chose a deep-green dress tonight. It sets off my pale skin and red hair and, without any makeup to cover them up, my freckles are on full display. I press my fingers lightly to the bridge of my nose. They were a feature I loved and then grew to hate, worn down by Ethan's constant criticism. He thought they looked *childish*.

With a huff, I drop my hands. "I don't give a fuck what he thinks. He doesn't matter and he's not here. I am, and I love them." Even as I say the words, part of me wants to hunch my shoulders and look around to make sure no one heard. I force them away from my ears and lift my chin. "I *love* them."

I will reclaim everything he tried to take from me. No matter how long it takes.

A soft knock on the door has my heart leaping into my throat. I hurry to open it and look up into Sol's dark eyes. He looks splendid, wearing some soft-looking pants that I think might actually be called breeches and a vest embroidered with bright thread. The vest catches my interest, and I lean forward without thinking. "What are these?" They're plants, but not ones I recognize. Then again, why would I? Even if they were plants in my world, I'm hardly someone who knows them on sight.

"Ah." He holds still as I run my fingers along the raised stitches. "It was a gift from my mother. They're some of the herbs and flowers sacred to our goddess."

"I see. Oh, I recognize this one! Hyacinth." I realize I'm still stroking him and drop my hand. My skin heats. "Sorry, I keep overstepping with you. I promise I'm not normally this rude."

He catches my hand in his and brings it up to press against his vest again. "If I didn't like it, I'd tell you. Never apologize for touching me, Briar. Never."

A thrill goes through me, even as I tell myself I'm being foolish. I've known Sol less than a week. Surely I'm not taking him at face value. The contract is the only reason I lightly drag my fingers tips over the embroidery before dropping my hands. "It's very beautiful."

"Thank you." He turns and, after a moment, reaches for my hand. "You look beautiful, too."

It's strange to walk down the hall with my hand clasped in Sol's much larger one. Maybe it should make me worried about being infantilized, but really I just feel safe. I think my instincts must have finally tapped out for good.

He guides me in a new direction when we reach the ground floor, heading away from the entrance and the library and back toward an arching doorway that leads into the garden. Or park. Or whatever it is.

The sun has long since set, and I'm delighted to see that the lights I could view from the bedroom window are actually flowers that glow faintly in the darkness in a variety of colors. "Oh wow."

"They're safe to touch."

I shoot him a grateful look and slip my hand from his so I can bend down and drag my finger over the petals of a pink one. It feels like any other flower I've touched, velvety and cool from the night air. I rub my fingers together, half expecting the glow to be present against my skin, but it's not. "I'm sure your world has its dangers, but so far, I've only found delights."

"It does have its dangers, yes." He reclaims my hand, and we resume walking down the rock path. "But I intend to keep you surrounded by delights."

I shoot a look at him, wondering if I imagined the insinuation in that last sentence. The lights play along his scales, making him look even more otherworldly than normal but in a really lovely way. "I'm sorry about earlier."

"So am I." He squeezes my hand. "I was trying to scare you, and I shouldn't have."

I'm suddenly thankful for the low light to hopefully hide my blush and the heat that rolls through me at the memory of what I did after I fled his presence. "I, ah, wasn't scared."

His tongue flicks out in a quick movement that I instantly recognize. I've seen the same thing with snakes in documentaries. Sol's hand flexes around mine. "I know."

Can he... Can he *taste* my desire? Or, wait, that doesn't make any sense. If he's like the reptiles of my world, then he's *scenting* it. That might actually be worse. My blush makes me light-headed. "Um, what?"

"I went to apologize immediately afterward." He doesn't look at me. "No matter what else is true, you're safe here, Briar, and I didn't want you to feel like you weren't. Especially not from me."

"Ah."

"I heard you. Scented you." Sol finally glances down at me. "I'll answer your questions tonight if you'd like."

I don't know whether to try to melt into the ground or make excuses or maybe just expire on the spot. The path ends before I decide. There's a cozy courtyard tiled with the same stone that the path is and even more glowing flowers around its perimeter. The trees seem to arch over the space a little, framing the full moon overhead. In the center, sits a square table with two chairs—a backless one for him and tall one with arms for me. Several candelabras give a bit more light to see by.

My chair is tall enough that I have to hop to get into it, and I think I hear a hissing laugh, but when I look, Sol's expression is carefully blank. "Do you have a lot of human visitors here?"

"You're the first in a very long time." He scoots in my chair and moves around the table to take his seat. "Azazel and his people keep their contracted humans close, so if one wants to, ah, sample their charms, one must travel to him. It pleases him to have us coming begging for the pleasure."

I don't know how I feel about that, so I set it aside. "Is it a fetish thing? The reason you want humans?" I press my hands to the table to keep from slapping them over my mouth. He said I could ask my questions. I will not be sorry for doing it.

I just might die of embarrassment in the process.

"No." He clears his throat. "I accepted Azazel's invitation the first time because I was curious, but that's not the reason I attended the auction, and it's not the reason I married you."

I recognize some of the food on the table from meals I've eaten previously and spoon a few of the dishes onto my plate. The goblet is filled with a spiced wine I find really pleasant. I take a quick sip. "Why did you marry me, Sol? I deserve to know the full truth, don't you think? Why not marry another dragon? I'm sure it would be less of a tightrope than we've been walking the last couple days." Bold. So bold. My heart races in a rhythm I can feel in my temples. It's a question, but it feels like a challenge, and experience says challenging men is dangerous.

Either I am safe with Sol, or I am not. My actions have nothing to do with it. His do.

He sits back and picks up his goblet, which is when I realize that, like the chair, mine has been sized to me. Because his fits perfectly in the palm of his hand. He studies me. "I originally intended to do exactly that. I was courting with the intent to marry, but my parents stepped in." He doesn't make me ask for clarification. "They had bigger plans for me than my individual happiness, and while I resented that for a time, in the end they were right. A leader's responsibility is to their people, not themselves."

I don't know how to parse out the history from those few sentences. "But why is a human so necessary?"

"I'm knowledgeable about my people's history, but I'm hardly an expert on biology, so forgive me if my explanation leaves something to be desired." He sips his drink, somehow making it look perfectly natural despite his non-human jaws.

"There's something about the biology or the inherent *something* of humans that makes you excellent conductors for magic, even if full humans don't possess it themselves."

A shiver works through my body, and I have to set down my drink. "So you're going to, what, experiment on me?" I'm proud of myself. The sentence comes out calm and unruffled.

"What? Of course not." His crest flares in obvious agitation. "I'm making a mess of this. No, let me back up and start at the beginning."

"Please do." I think I'm shaking, but I can't quite be sure. Of all the explanations I expected, *this* seems the most outlandish. Humans are *conductors?* What does that even mean?

Sol shakes his head, and his crest eases a little. "Our realm is steeped in magic, and the territories are linked to their individual leaders. The strength of the leader—and their magic—directly influences the strength of the territory's magic and the well-being of its people."

"Okay," I say slowly. It boggles my mind, but that's easy enough to follow. "Where do humans come into this?" I will reserve judgment until he finishes his explanation. I *will*.

"At some point in the distant past, it was discovered that breeding with humans boosted that magic. It was at a time when travel between the realms was more widespread. So we intermingled with humans, and that's partly why we all look the way we do now. But then the realms closed to each other, except for the bargainer demons, and each following generation became a little weaker, a little less magical."

I stare. This is both better and so much worse than what I was imagining. Easy enough to connect the dots now. "You don't need me, then. You need a child."

To his credit, he doesn't look away as he nods. "Our child will be the next ruler of this territory and, if they're half human, they will invigorate my people in way I am incapable of doing. Harvests haven't started to fail, but it's only a matter of time before we're unable to use magic to keep the soil fertile. No one's starving yet... But in a generation or two? They will."

I try to sympathize. I do. He's obviously carrying a burden beyond anything I can imagine. So many lives held in the balance. To be thinking of the future instead of attempting to curate his own power is a testament to the kind of person he is. I can appreciate that, even if I'm already shaking my head. "You want me to have a baby with you and then walk right out of their life in seven years. Do you realize what a big ask that is, Sol? I've already lost everything. You'll take this from me, too?"

He doesn't flinch or look away. "I'm sure we can find a way around that."

Around what? The seven-year deadline? Around the inability to cross realms without Azazel or one of his people involved? Even if I wanted to take the child back with me, if they look anything like Sol, we wouldn't last a month before someone attacked them or some government took them for experiments. Technology has made my world too small to effectively hide in. "The cost is too high," I whisper. I fumble for the goblet and take too large a drink. "It's not fair. You can't ask that of me."

"We have seven years, Briar. You don't have to answer tonight."

He *would* say that. What is *he* risking? "The answer won't change. It's no. No babies. Absolutely not."

CHAPTER 11

BRIAR

*D*inner passes in awkward silence. I realize I'm punishing Sol for telling me the truth, but that very truth is lodged in my throat. It doesn't matter how delicious the food or wonderful the drink. Sol wants my *baby*. I haven't even decided if I *want* children. It was a future I refused to share with Ethan, going so far as to get a birth control prescription and hide it from him to ensure I didn't bring a child into this world and under his control.

The idea of going back on that determination, only to pass the child off, never to be seen again, is unthinkable.

Sol rises suddenly. "I'll be right back. Please wait here." He strides out into the darkness before I have a chance to respond.

Now's the time to flee, to run back up to my bedroom and hide. Since I've arrived here, I've needled Sol and challenged him and infuriated him. He hasn't said so much as a sharp word in response. Yes, he detailed out exactly what he wants to do to me, but I can't pretend what he described isn't at least partially welcome. It'd be hypocritical in the extreme to do so after I touched myself to the fantasy of it.

71

If a baby weren't in the picture...

I take a hasty sip of my wine. I've nearly drained the glass, which should be worrisome, but I don't feel drunk in the least. Buzzed, maybe, but I can't blame the wine for that.

Sol appears on the other side of the courtyard, stepping out of the shadows as if he teleported in. His crest is half-raised, and it sinks when he catches sight of me. "You didn't leave."

I don't think I could have gotten to the edge of the garden in that amount of time. But he's right; I didn't even try. "You asked me not to."

He rounds the table and sinks to a knee next to me. With the height of my chair, the position means I can look directly into his dark eyes. They flicker strangely in the firelight of the candelabras. Sol holds up an arm. A thin chain hangs from his fist, a pendant swinging lightly with the motion. It's a simple thing, an oval with a strange symbol burned into it. "Here."

"Thank you," I say automatically.

He hisses a little. "Don't thank me until you know how it works." He cups my hand and sets the pendant on my palm. "This was passed along by Ramanu when they visited. A few drops of your blood will activate the spell. You'll need to reactivate it on the first day you start menstruating each month, but the pendant is good for decades."

I stare at the symbol and then lift my gaze to his. "What does it do?"

"As long as you wear it, you won't become pregnant." He closes my hand around the pendant. "You've only been here a few days, Briar. I realize my honesty is unwelcome, but I won't lie to you about what I want." He hesitates. "However, I'm willing to be patient."

A broken laugh rips from my mouth. "If you're telling the truth about this pendant, then why would I ever take it off? I could spend the next seven years fucking you and then go home without ever going through with having that baby you want so badly."

"Yes. You could."

I wait, but he simply holds my gaze. There's a challenge there, maybe, but I'm too dazed to think it through. "How can I trust that it works?"

"If you'd like it verified, you can ask Ramanu. *They* have no reason to lie to you."

I almost protest that of course they do, because my having a baby is part of the bargain.

But it's not.

The only thing the contract says it that Sol has the opportunity to seduce me, to attempt to accomplish his aim, but nowhere in either of them did it say I was required to get pregnant or give birth. Only that if I *did*, the child would remain in this realm.

Sol is telling the truth. I'm certain of it, even if I barely trust myself enough to believe him. I'm going to be here for seven years. Why wouldn't he think he has plenty of time to convince me to do what he wants?

The question remains: What do *I* want?

"Okay," I say slowly. "I believe you."

"Keep it around your neck. As long as the cord remains intact, it will continue to work."

I obediently slip it around my neck. The cord is long enough that the pendant hangs between my breasts. "Is there anything special that I need to do except bleed on it?"

"No."

I lift my hand, suddenly feeling bold and a little wild. "Will you lend me a tooth?"

He goes perfectly still, and my heart trills in response. The urge to run from this obvious predator is almost overwhelming, but somehow my fight-or-flight responses are all

73

tangled up with something rushed and heated. I will *not* give him what he wants, but maybe we can settle for a compromise. He wants me. He's not being subtle about it.

And me? I want him, too.

I never considered myself a reckless person, but I don't know what other word can describe me as Sol opens his mouth. His teeth are long, nearly half the length of my fingers and wickedly sharp. His tongue is forked. I have the strangest desire to stroke it, but I settle for reaching into his mouth an pressing the pad of my thumb to one of his teeth. Even knowing it's coming, I can't help sucking in a breath as the prick of pain.

I waste no time withdrawing and pressing my thumb to the pendant. It flares a bright green, and I feel an answering tug in my lower stomach. For all I know, I just made myself doubly fertile…but I don't think so.

It still takes far more courage—or recklessness—to say, "What if we tried it? Sex, I mean."

Sol's crest flares, the only move he makes. "Are you saying that because you want sex, or because you're running from something in your head?"

"Does it matter?"

"It should." He pushes slowly to his feet and holds out a hand. "But I want you, Briar. I won't pretend I don't."

I slide my hand into his and let out a little yip when he pulls me off the chair and into his arms. He's so warm that I whimper a little. Sol sets me on the table and clasps the back of my head with one massive hand. I have the almost-hysterical thought that he could crush my skull like a melon, but he holds me gently, if firmly. "Are you sure?"

No. "Yes."

Bless him, but he takes me at my word. "I'll buy you another dress."

I barely have time to process the words when he moves.

He rips my dress open with a single swipe of his claws. The fabric parts and flutters down on either side of my body, baring me completely. I didn't even have time to tense.

Sol stares down at me for a long moment and then meets my gaze. "If it's too much, say stop."

It's not quite a reassurance that my saying stop will be enough to *actually* stop him, but I can barely think past the hot grip on the back of my head and the warm breeze that caresses my newly bared skin. "Okay," I manage.

His forked tongue flicks out and caresses my bottom lip. I open for him. It doesn't even occur to me not to. His tongue strokes mine. It's not quite a kiss in the traditional sense of the word, but our jaws are hardly compatible for that kind of thing. Before I can decide it's awkward, he tilts me back and licks his way down my throat in sensual little flicks that make me shiver.

Sol pauses at my breasts and nuzzles me, like a cat scent-marking their owner. Then his tongue is at my nipples, remarkably agile as he tugs and toys with me. Each pull sends an answering one lower in my body.

I...don't know how to feel.

I honestly expected him to go for fucking me as quickly as possible. I want him badly enough that I don't mind the inevitable pain that would come with such a hurry. At least then I'd *know* if the reality was even close to what my mind had dreamed up. "Sol, please!"

"Don't rush me," he murmurs, his breath hot against my skin.

A quiet *snick* sound, and his claws detract. I stare. "I didn't know they could do that."

Sol doesn't respond, other than to sink to his knees before the table and push my thighs wide. I'm too shocked to do anything but quiver as he presses a single finger slowly into me, almost as if he's testing me. The sight... I don't know what to look at. It feels too personal to watch that large green finger penetrate my pussy. Looking at his face, at the intent way he watches me, is even worse.

I'm a coward.

I close my eyes.

The sensation only increases without the visuals to distract me. He's not hurting me, but I can't deny how full a single finger makes me feel. If he fucked me this quickly, he'd split me in half. My body pulses at the thought. I don't know why that turns me on. It doesn't make any sense. I hate pain. Why would I crave it like *this*?

Sol withdraws his finger, and my eyes fly open as I make an involuntary sound of protest. He catches my hips and jerks me half off the table, only his hold keeping me from tumbling to the ground.

And then he closes his mouth around me. His jaws are big enough that his teeth prick my lower stomach and my ass, tiny little flickers of pain that I barely feel because his tongue is at my entrance. He works it into me slowly. Unrelentingly.

I knew his tongue was large, of course—*everything* about him is large—but being penetrated by it is different. It feels as big as a cock, but it doesn't move inside me like a cock. It's agile and slick and— "Holy fucking shit."

He makes a hissing sound that somehow translates as pleasure instead of anger. It vibrates through his jaws to my lower body, and I can't help shivering in response. Then he goes after my G-spot again.

It has to be my G-spot. I've read novels. I looked up the existence of such a "magical" spot. I even went so far as to try to find it myself, but when one has limited time to mastur-bate, it's easier to just go with what works.

It's never felt like this.

Every bone in my body goes deliciously liquid. Even my thoughts stop swirling frantically. There's nothing but that steady pulse inside me and his fingers digging into my hips as his teeth prick my skin. "More."

Was that low demand from me? It hardly seems possible.

But I want more. I *need* it.

Within thinking, I reach down and grab his wrists. My fingers don't meet on the other sides, but that's fine. "Sol, *more*."

CHAPTER 12

SOL

I had intended to offer Briar the pendant and end the night there. She doesn't trust me, and I can hardly blame her for that. I'm not even certain what happened. One moment she was looking at me as if she wished she could read my mind, and the next I had her on the table and was ripping her dress off.

And now?

I hiss in pure pleasure as she grabs my wrists and rolls her hips, riding my tongue. She tastes like a dream. It's even better because she's mine. Not some otherwise-contracted human looking for a fun fuck and then going away at the end of the encounter.

No, Briar is my bride.

Mine.

Her thighs shake against my palms. "Sol. Oh god, oh god, I—" Her pussy pulses around my tongue, her orgasm tasting so good, I almost cum in my pants.

It takes far more effort than I'll ever admit to in order to unclench my jaw and withdraw from her. Her pussy is drenched, swollen and pink and dripping. I can't help myself. I drag my tongue over her again.

She moans and then tenses. Coming back to herself. I could keep this going. She's given me the keys to herself, even if she doesn't realize it. It was there in the shocked expression on her face when I went to my knees before her. This woman has never been properly cared for, and she's never had her pleasure prioritized.

But pushing her now means potentially sacrificing the endgame later. As tempting as it is, I'm mortal and not even I can keep her at a fever pitch for seven years. We have to eat at some point. My territory might require very little in the way of ruling—at least outside of dealing with trade agreements with the other territories and their leaders—but there is still all the damned paperwork to consider.

I can be the patient predator. I *will* be.

No matter how delicate her taste on my tongue or how sweet her cries of release.

There's no saving her dress, but she seems the type to be bothered by public nudity, even in the keep. I scoop her into my arms, careful to tuck the torn dress around her. I like how neatly she fits. I more than like how she melts against me and presses her cheek to my chest.

"Warm," Briar murmurs.

It's difficult to walk with my cocks hard enough to make me dizzy, but I manage. I can sense several of the staff waiting at the perimeter of the garden, but they wait until I've left the table to approach. It's just as well. I don't stand on ceremony, but right now I'm feeling...strange.

Is this the mating frenzy?

I've never experienced it before. I never got the chance to with Anika, for all that we were having plenty of sex during the official courtship. They were never *mine* in a way Briar is

79

as my wife. I was never *theirs* in the way their husband is now. We were simply enjoying each other and testing out the idea of forever.

I didn't think that distinction would make a difference. I thought our precautions were a bit over the top when Aldis first insisted on them, but now I'm grateful for her stubbornness. I don't know what I'd do if I saw another dragon while feeling like this.

I tighten my hold on Briar and lean down to inhale the scent of her. *Mine.* I pick up my pace. I will carry her back to her rooms—our rooms, really—and leave her there. The memory of her cumming around my tongue and the knowledge that she's sleeping in my bed, even if I'm not there to share it, will have to be enough to keep my control tightly leashed.

I will not spook her.

I refuse to.

But when I set Briar gently on her feet in front of the door and move to take a step back, she hooks her fingers into the waistband of my pants. "Wait. Don't go."

Pure lust surges, and it's everything I can do to keep it locked down. "You've had enough."

She looks up at me, her expression settling into something I don't recognize. It's hard and almost furious. She tugs on my waistband. "You don't get to decide that. I do."

My cocks go harder yet, and I clench my jaw. "You don't know what you're asking for."

"Don't I?" She takes an almost tentative step closer and presses her free hand to the front of my pants. She traces a line down one cock and then cups the other. "Please, Sol. I don't know if I'll have the courage to do this again if we don't finish it tonight."

Another indication that I'm taking advantage. If I were

half as honorable as everyone claims dragons are, I'd brush off her hold and walk away. It doesn't happen. Instead, my body moves almost of its own accord, and I reach past her to open the door.

Briar's brilliant smile is a reward in and of itself.

She steps back through the door, tugging me behind her. I follow, an obedient little pup fighting not to turn into a full predator and ravish her. I kick the door shut behind me. The room is too quiet, filled only with our mingled harsh breathing.

"I can't take both," she rushes to say. "But what we did before...That felt really good." Her hand trembles against my length. "Maybe this could feel good, too."

I try to slow down. To parse out her words. To come up with a suitable response that won't scare her silly.

It doesn't work. My brain has taken a back seat to desire. The only thing I can do is follow her lead, allowing her to pull me toward the bed. "I think I would like to meet this person who made you think sex shouldn't feel good." I can't help flexing my fists at my sides, my claws sliding out.

Briar glances down and raises her brows. "I don't think you'd like him much, but it's a moot point. He's dead."

Azazel's work, no doubt. I'll have to press the demon for details when I encounter him next. Details like how he spilled the bastard's guts all over the floor. He better have made Briar's ex suffer. It's the least he could do.

"All the same," I manage.

"I don't want to talk about him." She gives me one last tug, and I have the presence of mind to hook her around the waist as she tips back, rotating so I land on my back with Briar straddling my stomach. She blinks down at me. "You're so fast when you want to be."

"I'm trying not to frighten you," I grit out.

Briar tentatively runs her hands over my chest. "You... don't." She says it slowly, almost seeming to marvel over the revelation. "That's strange, isn't it? Even when I don't like what you're saying or what your goals are, I'm not really scared of you." She shakes her head, her red hair shining in the low light of the lamp by the desk. "I think I might really be a fool. I have no reason to trust you."

She's right, but it stings all the same. I start to sit up. "We're moving too fast."

"Stop that." She pushes against my chest, and it's almost absurd how weak she is. I could hold this position indefinitely, but I allow her to urge me down onto my back. Her claw-less fingers knead at my scales. "Unless you don't want this? It's okay if you don't."

"Briar." Her name comes out almost as a curse. "I am doing everything in my power not to lose control right now. Have mercy."

Her slow smile has my cocks practically bursting out of my pants. "Mercy," she echoes. "Sol, you truly are a surprise on every level, aren't you? I would like to take off your pants now."

"Do it."

She fumbles my belt open and then gets tangled trying to pull the fabric past my thighs and tail. I give a frustrated curse and wrap one arm around her to shift her higher so I can use the other to shred through my pants.

I liked those pants, but I like settling Briar back onto my lower stomach without anything between us even more. She shrugs out of her ruined dress, leaving the fabric to flutter to the ground beside the bed. She glances over her shoulder, and her pale skin goes a rather fetching pink. "Two," she says faintly. "And so big."

The faint tremor in her voice has me digging my claws into the bedding to avoid reaching for her. "You lead."

She finally looks back at my face. "Lead?"

"Yes." A hiss works into my voice, but I can't help it. Her pussy is slippery against my scales; she says I'm the warm one, but she's *scorching* me.

The moment spins out between us. A small line appears between her brows, but she finally comes to some conclusion and nods. "Okay. I can do this." She inches off me and awkwardly maneuvers around to perch on my thighs. "I *want* to do this."

Her body frames my cocks, and even having been with humans before, I can't stop the surge of sheer lust at the thought of sinking into her body. Will she be able to take all of me? I don't know. The not knowing *torments* me. I need to find out. I need to press into her tight, wet sheath and feel her clamp around me.

I need...

Briar wraps both her hands around the head of my lower cock, and my thoughts short out. She touches me slowly, exploring me in a way that makes me want to roar. *Touch me. Harder.* I clamp my jaws shut to keep the orders inside. She's not like the others I've been with. I am her first of my kind, and no doubt the first of my size. I have to go slow. To prepare her. To check—

She dips down and drags the flat of her tongue over my slit. I nearly cum right then and there. The sensation only gets stronger when she sits back and licks her lips. "I...I can't take you in my mouth. Not properly."

Goddess, but this woman is going to kill me.

I tighten my grip on the bedding, the faint shredding sound making her look at me in askance. "Don't stop," I bite out. "I'm fine."

"You don't look fine." She coasts her fingertips down the top of one cock and up the underside of the other. "You look like you're in pain." A tiny smile tugs at the edges of her lips, but her dark eyes are troubled. "Will you lose control?"

"No." The word is so garbled, it doesn't sound like me.

"Are you sure?"

I can't tell if she's teasing me or it's a genuine question. *Goddess, give me strength. I. Will. Not. Frighten. Her.* "I give you my word. I won't lose control. This time."

CHAPTER 13

BRIAR

*T*his time.

I have never felt more powerful than I do in the moment when I give one of Sol's two—*two*—cocks a stroke and watch every muscle stand out in his body. I've never put much thought into the attractiveness of cocks, but his are lovely. They just like the rest of him, humanoid and yet not at the same time. They both curve slightly toward his stomach and they're a deep green.

He's absolutely shredding the bed with his claws, as if he needs *some* outlet. As if my fumbling, tentative touches are enough to drive this dragon to distraction.

I shouldn't tease him. He's obviously holding on by a thread, and while the idea of being so tempting as to make him lose control is an attractive one, the sheer size of his cocks is enough to give me pause. I don't know if I can take *one*, let alone both. The thought of forcing it makes my stomach drop out.

It's been good with him. Pleasurable. I don't want that to stop.

It's more than that, though. He's given me pleasure, yes,

but he's also given me other things that are equally valuable. Honesty. Patience. A kind of caring that I can barely comprehend. I'm not naïve enough to think that it will always be like this, but at the same time, how can I not be entirely seduced by the idea of spending the next seven years as this man's wife?

"Briar."

I drag my gaze back up to meet his. His features may not be human, but his eyes are easy enough to read now that I've spent a little time with him. They're practically burning with need. I press my palm to the pendant that hangs between my breasts, and he follows the movement with a slight jerk that's more reptilian than human. "The spell will work. You're protected."

Even now, he's reassuring me that I'm safe. Protected. The pendant feels nearly as warm against my skin as his body does. I look down at his cocks again and swallow hard. "How do I do this?"

Sol hisses in what sounds like agony. "Take the bottom. Rub yourself on the top."

He's done this before, I remind myself. The thought pricks like needles in my skin. He's taken care of others before me. Ensured they felt good and safe and... No reason for me to feel jealous of some faceless human who's had him before. Even if they were more experienced and probably didn't need to be handled with kid gloves the way he's treating me right now. I bet he fucked them instead of lying there and letting them fumble their way through the process.

"Briar."

Every time he says my name, it's as if he reaches right into the heart of me and strokes something soft and sinful. I drag in a breath and lift myself up until I'm able to notch his massive cock at my entrance. "You're too big."

He curses, his voice strained and sibilant. "Relax. Let your body and gravity do the work."

Relax? I'm about to be torn in half. I give a half-hysterical laugh. "I don't know who you were having sex with before, but they must be better at this than me. I *can't* take you."

He grabs my hips. His hands are so big, they encompass me entirely. Sol bends up and flicks his tongue over my nipples. "You *can* take me, bride." He presses me down, the broad head of his cock breaching me. "You were made for me."

I can't think past the sheer invasion of him. I shift my hips, but he doesn't let me escape. He doesn't shove up into me or try to rush things, but I can't escape him. My breath sobs out. "It's too much."

He pauses. "Do you want to stop?"

"*No.*" The denial comes quick and harsh. This whole experience is overwhelming, but it's not bad. Not even a little bit.

"Then take my other cock in your hand," he commands.

I obey immediately. He feels just as absurdly large against my palm as he does in my pussy. I look down and give a harsh laugh. "You're barely inside me."

"I'm aware," he grits out.

"It's—"

"Rub my cock on that hungry little clit, Briar. Do it now."

I jolt at the harsh command in his voice, which makes me sink a little farther down his length. He still feels impossibly large. I tentatively press his other cock to my clit, feeling silly. What is this? "*Oh.*" He's so soft here. I knew that, of course. I had my hands and mouth on him a short time ago. But the hardness is what has me shivering as if I'm having an out-of-body experience. I squeeze his cock as I press him back to my clit again.

It feels good, but I need...

I move my hips a little. *Yes. That's what I need. Friction.* I press him harder to my clit and roll my hips. Distantly, I'm aware of the fact that I'm sinking farther down his cock with each stroke, but all I feel is pleasure in the midst of overwhelming fullness.

"There you go." Sol's voice is distorted. "Take me, bride. Make yourself feel good."

"It's too much," I whisper. But my body knows what my mind doesn't. There's no hesitation. I ride him slowly, working myself down until I can't take any more of him.

His grip shifts down to cup my ass. I barely register what he's doing until he tenses, and then suddenly my weight is in the palm of his hands. I start to protest, but he lifts me, easing me nearly off his cock. "No! I need it."

Sol's hissing laugh makes my pussy flutter. "I'll give you what you need." He lowers me, one agonizingly slow inch at a time. "You need to cum all over this cock."

I can hardly reconcile this filthy-speaking lover with the courteous—if blunt—dragon I've been getting to know. I don't know what it says about me that I *like* the scandalous words he spills. I like that he moves me around like... "Make me. Fill me up." I don't mean to say the words out loud, but it's a habit I'm developing with Sol that I don't know how to stop.

"What?" Sol says slowly.

This isn't real, I think dazedly. *Nothing I say matters. This is out of time, out of space. It's all pretend.* If it's all pretend...then maybe I can say the sinful, unforgivable words bubbling up behind my lips. I can't stop shaking. I'm so close, I feel feverish. "I want you to fuck me, Sol. I want you to fill me up with your seed, just like you promised. I—" I swallow hard. The words are crass and taking things too far. I don't know what's wrong with me, but it's like I can't stop. I should be ashamed. I want to be valued and cherished and yet... "Make me feel good."

A shudder works through his body, and his grip on my ass tights, his claws pricking my skin. "I am *trying* not to scare you."

I know. That's why I feel safe enough to do this. I stroke down his upper cock, doing my best to hold his gaze. I need to know how far this goes. He's trying to hold back, and while I deeply appreciate that, I also want to get under his skin just as much as he's gotten beneath mine in such a short time. "Promise me this pendant will work."

His breath hisses out. "It will work. I promise."

"Make me cum," I whisper. I lick my lips. "Fill me up."

"Fill you up." He arches up until our faces are even. "What a little fucking tease you are, Briar." I tense, but he's not saying it like it's a bad thing.

Still… "I'm sorry?"

"No, you're not." He loops his forearm around my waist, and then we're moving. Sol easily climbs off the bed without dislodging me from his cock and turns to set me down on the edge of the bedding. He leans over and presses his hands down on either side of my head, staring at my splayed body. "You like to make me crazed."

He's right. I do.

I like it even better when he starts moving, fucking into me in slow strokes that never go too far. I press down on his top cock, so that he's fucking against my body. It feels so good, my back bows.

"My bride." He thrusts a little harder. Testing me. "You've got a needy little pussy, don't you? Is that enough cock for you, Briar?"

"No." I shake my head against the bedding. What felt like too much only a short time ago is suddenly exactly right. "I can take more, Sol. Please."

"You're a good girl, Briar." His voice does that sibilant thing that curls my toes. "A good girl for everyone else. Not

89

for me, though." He nuzzles my throat, his teeth dragging lightly over my vulnerable skin. "For me, you'll take every inch and ask for more." He thrusts deeper.

"Yes!"

"Tight little pussy practically begging me to fill you up." He hardly sounds like he's speaking to me. His words blur together until they're nearly incomprehensible. He traces the pendant cord with his tongue, and for one breathless moment, I think he means to bite it right off. I'm so far gone, I might cum on the spot if he did.

Sol doesn't, though. He promised, after all.

He picks up his pace. I can tell he's still being careful with me, but not nearly as careful as he was up to this point. Each stroke makes my breasts bounce and steals the breath from my lungs. "Cum, Briar. Right fucking now."

Pleasure surges, sending me closer to the edge, but it's not enough. "I can't," I sob. I try to move, to meet his thrusts, but I'm pinned too effectively.

"Fill you up," he mutters. "Put a baby in you."

"No." But I lift my hips to take him deeper. "You won't."

Sol's hissing laugh is almost cruel. Almost…but not quite. "Then tell me to stop. Because if you don't, I'm going to cum inside you, bride." His stroke hitches, losing its smooth rhythm. "And if I fill you up, I'm never going to stop. Do you understand me? Every chance I get, you're going to be on my cock. One and then the other."

"I—" Whatever I was about to say ends in a startled scream as he thrusts deep. It feels like he's pounding against the end of me, each spurt from his bottom cock a throbbing contact even as his cum overflows my pussy.

Sol barely waits for the spurts to stop before he jerks out of me and then fills me with his second cock. "Take it, bride. Take it all." He thrusts deep a second time, and it's too much. I scream my way through an orgasm even as he follows, filling me...*over*filling me...and then slumping down onto his side and taking me over with him, his cock still twitching inside me.

I come back to myself in waves. A deep kernel of pleasure still throbs inside me, and I have the mildly horrified thought that it wouldn't take much for me to turn back into that scandalous woman demanding Sol fuck me and fill me.

Who *was* she?

He pulls me closer, and I try to mind the fact that I'm soaked from the waist down or that I am going to be incredibly sore as soon as the endorphins wear off. I try... And I fail.

"Too much?" he finally asks.

God, but I *like* this dragon. I nuzzle his scaled chest and then jump when his cock twitches inside me. "Stop that. I can't take any more."

"You'll take what I give you." But there's no urgency behind the statement. "Answer the question, Briar."

Once again, I find myself grateful for our size difference because it makes it easy not to meet his gaze while I tell the truth. "No," I whisper. "It wasn't too much." And then, because he asked, I can't help but do the same. "Was *I* too much?"

Sol trails a single claw down my spine. "Never." He eases me off his cock and moves me up until our faces are even, erasing my ability to hide from him. His dark eyes are oh so serious as he studies me. "Bedroom games are what they are." He drags one giant thumb along the underside of one breast. "I promised I won't remove the pendant, and I won't. But if you want to play pretend breeding games in the bedroom? I am more than happy to." He circles my nipple with a claw, the touch featherlight. "Or the study. Or the library. If you need me to lead this, Briar, that I am all too happy to play with you." He pauses. "At least as long as you want it."

I swallow hard. "And if I want to stop?"

"Then we will stop."

Again, I can't help thinking that Sol is too good to be true. But then, he's not, is he? No matter how much I'm starting to enjoy my time with him, that time has an end date in mind. Seven years. The thought almost makes me laugh. I haven't even been here seven *days*, and I barely recognize myself. What will it be like in a few months? In a few years?

I thought for certain Sol wouldn't have a chance to convince me to do what he wants, but I feel like another person when I'm having sex with him. Who will I be if we keep on like this?

CHAPTER 14

BRIAR

Sol palms me between my thighs. "Are you sore?"

"A little." Possibly more than a little. He's not small, and he wasn't overly gentle toward the end. I try to close my legs, and I flinch. "Okay, yes. Very."

He does that really cute nuzzling thing along my jaw, and then he's up and moving. "Stay there."

I couldn't move if I wanted to. My legs won't stop shaking, and the little tremors work north through my body. It's not unpleasant, but it's disconcerting in the extreme to have lost control of my limbs.

Sex has never been like this before.

I press my hand to my mouth to stifle a laugh. *Of course, it's never been like this before. I just had sex with a dragon.* Except it's more than that. Sol put my pleasure first. He didn't use my loss of control to demean me. I'm pretty sure he could call me a dirty little slut, and I'd enjoy it because from him, it would sound like a compliment the same way *bride* does. I don't understand it, but I'm too floaty to question it.

He returns and pauses at the edge of the bed, staring down at me. It's then that I realize his penises are gone. I

93

stare hard at his hips. Did the scales there split earlier? I can't remember. I struggle up onto my elbows, but that's about all I'm capable of right now. Better to look at his face than wonder where his cocks have gone. Safer, maybe. "I can't read your expression. What are you thinking?"

He hesitates but finally gives himself a shake. "I'm thinking that you're mine, Briar Rose."

Okay, maybe not safer. I tense, waiting for the instinctive denial. I know what it is to be with a partner who thinks they can claim me as a possession instead of a person. It…doesn't come. Still, I lift my chin. "I'm *mine*, Sol."

"Yes." He bends down and scoops me into his arms. "But you're also mine." He turns and carries me into the bathroom. The oversized tub is full of steaming water, and Sol just walks right into it. Suddenly, it's not oversized at all. I tense, but he settles back against the edge and bands a forearm across my waist. "Relax. The hot water will help with soreness."

The endorphins from the multiple orgasms are starting to wear off. *Soreness* might be the understatement of the century. Every muscle hurts as if I've run a marathon, but I don't think marathon runners have a throbbing between their legs. Then again, what do I know?

I gingerly brush my fingers to the little cuts that line my lower stomach. I can feel a matching set on my ass. "You bit me."

He hisses out something resembling a laugh. "If I truly bit you, I don't think you'd survive it."

"Probably not." I relax back against him, letting the water buoy me even as Sol holds me steady. "What do you do for fun, Sol? When you're not running this territory or visiting Azazel to fuck his humans?"

"You make it sound as if they're his pets." He snorts. "And, beyond that, I've only visited a handful of times."

"Do you fuck a lot of dragons then?" God, why am I asking this? That jealousy from before is back and burning a hole in my chest.

He pauses as if weighing his response. "I have hardly been celibate since reaching maturity, even after my courtship ended. There were several dragon partners over the years, and we always had a mutual understanding about what our relationships could and couldn't be."

Because his parents wanted him to marry a human and save the territory. The knowledge makes me feel strange. "I..."

"Don't stop speaking your thoughts now." His forearm flexes against my hips. "Tell me what you're thinking."

"I don't want to share you," I whisper. "I can see why you'd prefer a dragon, especially since you almost married one, but if you're my husband and I'm your wife, then I want to be exclusive." Funny how I've gone from not wanting to be married again to demanding the dragon husband I never wanted to be only with me.

Sol nuzzles my temple. "There will be no one else but you, Briar. I promise."

Another promise I have no business believing, but he's given me no reason to doubt him. I stare at the stone wall, wondering how we got into such uncharted waters so quickly. He's tense at my back, and coward that I am, I divert us back to safer topics. "Are you sure the humans *aren't* Azazel's pets?"

He relaxes against me. "They're free enough, even if they remain in bargainer demon territory. I can't speak to their motivations, but they're hardly kept caged and passed around without consent. Not all of them choose to, ah, entertain Azazel's guests from other territories."

I trace a finger along his scales. Yes, better to talk about Azazel than the strangely territorial feeling coursing beneath my skin. "If he has that many humans, why did he have to bring in us five for you? Why not just let them intersperse with the rest of the realm's population?"

"Azazel is a canny bastard." He huffs out a breath. "It's intentional. We might be at peace now, but we haven't always been. He dangles a tempting fruit in front of us and withholds the true possibility of more than just a taste. The presence of so many humans when travel between the realms is rare is a tempting fruit, but Azazel's lineage is littered with humans. He's significantly more powerful than the rest of us, and as a result, his territory will never be conquered."

This world is recognizable in some ways, but so foreign in others. "The balance seems to work well enough in this realm. You're not at war."

"Not currently." He sighs. "I won't lie and say I'm not concerned about what will happen if some territory leaders succeed and others fail. Our skirmishes have been just that for several generations. Skirmishes. But if the balance were to tip in a substantial way, war is all but inevitable."

I shiver. Obviously I knew a child was part of Sol's goals, but I hadn't paused to consider the implications that all the territory leaders might be out for the same thing. Except… "But about the smoke and fire lady? How does that work with, uh, pregnancy and stuff?"

"Rusalka." He says her name almost like a curse. "The succubi and incubi don't choose leaders the same way the dragons do. It's not lineage that determines who inherits the title. It's strength."

"Oh." And a half-human child would be strong. I shudder. These territory leaders can't force us, but will the others hold out?

Hopefully they're doing a better job of it than I am.

Except that's not fair. I know where my line is, at least in that. I can't extend that to anyone but me. If one of the other women wants to have twelve babies with her monster, that's her business.

Even if it hurts Sol?

I shut the thought down. Hard. I made my deal with eyes wide open, but I didn't do it to help anyone else except me. I'm certainly not selfless enough to give up a child. I shiver again and wrap my hand around the pendant, letting its solidity steady me as much as having Sol wrapped around my tired body. "It seems very complicated."

"Yes."

I like that he's rather blunt. He doesn't play with words and talk circles around me. Even when he obviously doesn't want to talk about something, he doesn't make me feel like it's *my* fault that the subject came up and now he's irritated because I'm too dense to understand the problem.

I tense and slap the water. "Damn it."

"What's wrong?"

"It's like he's haunting me. I can't stop comparing the two of you, can't stop my expectations that things will be just as messed up with you as they were with him."

He rests his chin lightly on the top of my head. "I won't pretend to know your experiences, but I would imagine that something like that doesn't simply disappear because we'd like it to."

I glare at the tiled wall of the bathroom. "I want it to go away. He had power over me for far too long. I won't let him have more now that he's gone. Not anymore."

Silence except for our low breathing and the steady beat of Sol's heart thrumming through his chest where I rest my head. Finally, he says, "Would you like to see the library tomorrow? The translation spell only works for speaking, but I believe there's another that will allow you to read."

I sit up so fast, he has to jerk back to avoid me slamming into his jaw. "We could do that?" I'd wondered if it was possible, but with everything else that's happened since, I'd all but forgotten.

"I'll reach out to Azazel tomorrow with the request."

I turn in his arms, and he allows it. Maybe one day it will stop feeling so strange that I feel safer with a dragon with teeth and claws that could rip me to shreds than I've ever felt with a human. "I know the translation spell is very useful, but if I'm going to be here for seven years, I would like to learn your language properly."

He stares at me for a long time. "You know that's not necessary."

I start to tense, but he's being very careful with me in a way that isn't familiar. I sit up, perched on his thighs, and push my hair back. "I know it's not necessary, but that doesn't mean I don't want to do it." I don't know if our mouths being shaped so differently will make it an impossible task, but he's being so kind to me, and I want to know more about him. This isn't for a week or even a month. This is *seven years*. I can't spend all that time hiding away in a room. I want to know more about Sol and his people and their history. *Our* history, really, because there was overlap at some point in the distant past.

I cock my head to the side. "We have stories about dragons in my realm. But they don't look like you. They were as big as houses. Had a thing for virgins."

"Slander." Amusement filters into his tone. "If we took virgins, it was only because that's what your people offered. It wasn't preference."

It seems to defy possibility that dragons really did exist, but then again it defies possibly that I made a bargain with a demon and ended up in a different realm. "Are there still dragons that size?"

"Yes." He sifts his claws through my hair. "Some of our ancestors chose not to interbreed with humans, so there are still dragons as big as houses." Again, I get the faint strain of amusement, though he's definitely not laughing at me.

I think about. Then I think about it some more. "How did they…"

Sol gives that glorious hissing laugh of his. "Records are unclear, but after watching the bargainer demons and the incubi and succubi manage to breed, the less humanoid races made attempts as well."

Curiosity has me in a chokehold, but exhaustion rises in a tide I can't fight. "I'm going to have a thousand questions tomorrow."

"I look forward to it." For his part, he actually sounds like he means it. "I'd like to sleep with you tonight, Briar."

I should probably tell him no. Sex is one thing but… *But what?* I'm not someone who knows how to separate sex and emotion. I simply don't. I've been with exactly two other people in my history, and both were long-term boyfriends. I shudder. Neither were particularly good men, though.

But Sol isn't a regular man, is he? He's a dragon.

My emotions are already compromised. I won't allow that to change my mind about having a child with him and subsequently leaving them behind at the end of this bargain, but I've already suffered through so much. Heartbreak in seven years is a faint threat.

Heartbreak.

I almost laugh. Trust me to dive forward into the worst-case scenario. I like Sol, yes. I trust him in a fledgling kind of way. That hardly means I love him. "Yes, we can sleep together."

I very intentionally don't think about the fact it feels like I've just signed away far more than seven years.

CHAPTER 15

SOL

My bride suffers from nightmares.

I already resigned myself to a sleepless night. The cost is more than worth the reward of resting beside Briar. I'm a ruthless bastard, because I will take every inch she gives me and then push for more. I *like* my little redheaded bride. She's the strangest mix of brittle and strong, of afraid and more courageous than a beast four times her size. And when pleasure makes her forget to think so hard?

I have to focus on breathing to control my body's response. She'll need the balm the bargainer demons keep on hand for their humans. Something I should have considered when I was last in Azazel's presence.

That's when she whimpers.

It's a sound filled with absolute terror. I tense, immediately searching the room for a threat, but of course there's nothing. I would have noticed the moment something trespassed into my immediate territory. Not even the incubi or succubi with their smoke forms would be able to fool my senses. Not here.

Briar whimpers again. Her lips form into a near-soundless word. "*No.*"

I reach for her but stop short. Nightmares are strange creatures. Sometimes waking is the answer, but sometimes it makes things worse. I don't know which side of things Briar falls into. I hadn't thought to ask.

Helpless frustration rises with every twitch, with every wounded-animal sound she makes. *Haunted.* That's what she called herself. It's easy to forget during our waking hours when she's doing her best to charge forward in a way that's so sweet, it makes my teeth ache.

She found my presence comforting before. Perhaps it's enough to ward off the worst of her nightmares. At this point, lying here and waiting her out is all but impossible. If I were one of the incubi, I could slip into her dreams and fight whatever threatens her there. Even bargainer demons have more power in this kind of situation than I do, though they can only dream-hop if they have some incubi in their family history. Unfortunately, I'm constrained to the physical.

I turn onto my side, facing her, allowing my weight to dip the bedding between us. She slides closer. Another shift, and she's pressed against my chest. That should be enough, but I can't stop myself from shifting my tail over her thighs and against her back, urging her closer yet. Wrapping her up in me. Briar gives one last exhausted little sigh, and then she appears to fall into a dreamless slumber.

I don't sleep at all.

It's only when dawn creeps across the sky outside the window that I slip from the bed. I pause to tuck the blankets more firmly around her and get dressed. Then I duck out of the room and stride down the hall. There isn't a permanent portal open between the keep and Azazel's castle, but we have an open correspondence, courtesy of my previous visits.

Hopefully I can get this errand finished and be back before Briar wakes.

My study is exactly as I left it...except for the giant pile of paperwork that seems to have bred overnight. I know damn well if I hadn't sent away Aldis's assistants and staff, it wouldn't be so bad, but the mating frenzy is looking more likely in the cold light of morning. It's better for everyone that Briar and I find our feet without an audience.

What if we never find our feet?

I ignore the doubt threatening to worm through my brain and jerk open the top drawer. There is the scroll I bargained hard with Azazel to gain possession of. I have to force myself to slow down, to be gentle, as I pick it up and unroll it on the only clear part of the desk. It's magic, but that doesn't mean it's indestructible.

It takes a few seconds to scrawl out my request. I tap my claws on the desk, waiting for the reply. Azazel—or whoever he has monitoring communications—doesn't make me wait long. The reply comes in two minutes later.

I'll send Ramanu.

I glare at the words, but they don't change no matter how little they please me. Ramanu is an irritation, and they'll take one look at me and Briar and know exactly how far our relationship has escalated. Which they'll promptly report back to Azazel.

But if they bring the spell and the balm, I suppose that's a fair enough price to pay.

I stare at my desk for several long moments, but it's quickly apparent that I won't be concentrating on anything while I wait for Ramanu to arrive. More, I don't like having left Briar alone in bed. What we have feels fragile and easily shattered. She trusted me last night, and I won't do anything to endanger that.

The problem is that all my knowledge of humans comes

from limited interactions and books older than any dragon currently alive. Our people have changed significantly in the intervening generations. No doubt the humans have as well. I don't know enough, which means missteps are all but assured.

I shove to my feet and stalk out of the office. Better to be there when she wakes. Better not to backslide or give her time to doubt what happened between us. If I'd been thinking clearly, I never would have let things spiral so out of control, but I stopped thinking the moment I had my hands on her, and when I tasted her…

It was all instinct. I'm still not certain if instinct guided me in error or not.

Seven years felt a small eternity when I agreed to Azazel's bargain, but as I open my door and step through to find Briar curled up in my bed, I'm struck by the thought that it won't be nearly enough time at all.

I stalk to the bed and sink to perch on the edge. Her eyes flutter open, and I'm not keen on the lurching in my chest when they focus on me and she immediately smiles. It's a soft expression. Our faces are so different, our emotional tells so foreign to each other, but she's not adept at hiding hers. Not when I look into her dark eyes.

My bride is happy to see me this morning.

I reach out and carefully sift my claws through her tangled hair. "You were dreaming last night."

"Ah." Immediately, her expressive eyes close down. "I would rather not talk about it."

Which meant she was dreaming of *him*. I've never hated a stranger the way I hate Briar's late husband. It's an effort to keep my crest from flaring, to keep the hiss out of my voice. "Of course. But if you ever decide that talking might help, I'm here."

"Okay." She tentatively reaches up and runs her fingers

along my forearm, almost as if she can't believe she's allowed to touch me. That lurching feeling in my chest gets worse.

Briar clears her throat. "That bath last night was lovely, but I'm still going to be walking funny today. I am, uh, very sore."

"Ramanu should be here shortly with a balm that will help significantly." I only know how it works in theory, as the bargainer demons caretake their humans and don't allow anyone else to participate. Now that I have Briar, I understand a bit more. I'm not the sharing type, but if I were, I would want to have the softer moments in the aftermath for me and me alone.

"Ramanu."

She says it with such exasperation that I laugh. "Come, Briar. Let's get you fed, and hopefully that demon arrives before too long. Do you want me to carry you?"

She opens her mouth, hesitates, and finally seems to make herself meet my gaze. "Is it terrible that I kind of like that you carry me?"

"If it's terrible, then we're both terrible."

Briar smiles again. "I think I can make it to the bathroom alone, though."

She does, though it's mildly painful to watch her do it. I'm going to have to buy a vat of the healing balm if we're to have sex anywhere near as often as I'd like. I close my eyes and focus hard to get my body under control in the wake of that thought. There will be time for that later. Right now, I have a bride to feed and take care of.

Strangely enough, the thought is just as pleasant as the idea of sex. More so, even.

CHAPTER 16

BRIAR

$\mathcal{B}$y the time I make it out of the bathroom, I'm ready to tell Sol that I was too rushed in agreeing to be carried. What am I, a princess waiting for her knight in shining armor? Walking is mildly painful, but I've dealt with worse for less pleasurable reasons.

He never gives me the chance.

Sol waits near the door as if he's sure I'll collapse the moment I step through, a luxurious robe hanging from his claws. It's a deep green that matches the darkest part of his scales, and the material reflects the pale morning light in a way that makes my breath catch. He drapes it around my shoulders and waits for me to slide my arms through the generous sleeves. I belt it and shiver. The inside is even softer than it looks on the outside. Warmer, too. "Thank you."

"I like you in green." He sweeps me up into his arms without another word.

It feels different to be carried by him today. Now I know exactly what pleasure he's capable of delivering. My body clenches in response to the memory of last night that cascades over me. Which makes pain throb between my legs.

He really is massive, but even as sore as I am, I'm looking forward to doing it again. The sheer freedom of being with Sol, of not worrying that he's judging or going to hold anything I say in a moment of need against me...and that he's going to deliver *pleasure*. More pleasure than I could have dreamed possible.

What happened after the sex was just as revolutionary. He didn't roll over and immediately go to sleep. Or, worse, leave. He took care of me. And then he slept next to me, his larger body curled around mine. It might not have been enough to stave off nightmares, but that would take a miracle at this point.

It was nice. More than nice.

Sol tastes the air with his tongue. "What are you thinking of, Briar?"

Heat surges beneath my skin, and I suspect I've just turned as red as my hair. "Nothing."

"Liar."

I tense, but he says it almost fondly. I don't understand how Sol can use the same words Ethan did but for it to feel so different. I swallow hard. "I'm hungry."

He snorts and turns at the bottom of the staircase, heading deeper into the keep. I relax into his arms and enjoy the ride, but something occurs to me as Sol shoulders through a door and into a massive kitchen. A massive *empty* kitchen. "Why isn't there anyone else around? Surely you don't live here only with the brown dragon. There were more than a few dragons when I got here, but they're all gone now."

Sol sets me on a high stool and moves what appears to be a form of chest freezer. "My cousin, Aldis is around here somewhere. You met her the first day, and she's no doubt creating paperwork as we speak. There's also a small staff keeping us fed and ensuring the place doesn't fall down around us."

I frown. "It seems rather lonely."

Sol hesitates and then sets a series of strange-looking vegetation on the table. "The keep is usually more populated. I tend to make myself available to any of my people who need my attention, but they're forbidden from coming here for a time."

I worry my bottom lip, tempted to leave it at that, but Sol seems fine with my curiosity, so I gather up my courage and ask, "Why?"

His tail twitches, but his crest remains lowered. I'm not sure what that means, but it's not anger. He does seem to have a hard time meeting my gaze, though. "We dragons are territorial in the extreme, especially when newly wed. It's better for everyone if others make themselves scarce until the most intense time passes."

I blink. Blink again. "But what about the staff you just mentioned?"

"They're all old enough to have gone through this sort of thing several times, most recently with my parents." He shakes his head. "And Aldis is my cousin. Which doesn't make her exempt, but she's not interested in sex or marriage or anything of that nature, so we took a calculated risk having her here."

I don't know what to think about that. It almost sounds like a jealous rage, but Sol obviously took meticulous steps to ensure very few people were potentially endangered by it. "So if I were to talk to another dragon…"

His crest flares, a deep hiss rattling in his chest. "I suggest you don't. Not for the next few weeks." He takes a deep breath, and then another, visibly bringing himself under control again. "It will pass. It always does. But the initial time can be challenging, and I would appreciate it greatly if you worked with me on it. I realize humans don't have the same tendencies."

Don't we?

Maybe it's not as explicitly stated the way the dragons do, but humans can be wildly jealous, and it doesn't always wear off once they're secure in a relationship. I comb my fingers through my hair as Sol starts preparing the food. I'm not a jealous person. I couldn't afford to be, not with Ethan controlling every aspect of my life.

If Sol were with another person...

My stomach twists and my chest clenches. "I meant what I said last night. I don't want you with anyone else," I blurt. Maybe I should be playing cool or pretending like I don't care, but I can't seem to keep my cards close to my chest when it comes to Sol.

He walks to me, setting a plate of food in front of me. Too much food, honestly. Sol leans against the counter and waits until I pick up a piece of fruit that I recognize from yesterday's breakfast and take a bite. Only then does he speak. "There will be no one else, Briar. Even if I didn't hold marriage to be particularly sacred..." He shakes his head slowly. "No one else will do. It's you and no other."

Even as I try to tell myself he's only saying that because I'm his bride and I'm human and he needs to convince me to breed with him, part of me can't help melting at the sincerity in his words. To distract myself I take another bite and speak the thing that's been bothering me since last night. "I don't understand you."

"How so?"

"You are so courteous and kind when we talk like this." I motion between us. "But when it comes to sex, you're...different."

He shifts closer, and I jump a little when his tail spirals

around my leg. He leans down until our faces are even. "Did you like what we did last night?"

A shiver nearly dislodges me from the stool. It takes me two tries to find my words. "Yes." I lift my chin, barring my throat to him. "I…" I don't want to talk about Ethan, but at the same time, Sol is offering me a way to reclaim something I didn't realize I'd lost in the first place. "Sol, I like it when you talk to me like that. It feels like you're doing it in a way that's not *mean*."

It's so tempting to leave it there, but it's as if his presence propels honesty out of me. I swallow hard. "You make me feel cherished."

"You *are* cherished." He starts to say something else, but the sound of footsteps has him taking a slow step back.

No, not back.

He moves between me and the doorway.

I blink at his broad back for a long moment, but curiosity gets the best of me. I lean sideways just in time to see Ramanu stalk around the corner. They stop short. It's difficult to tell without them having eyes, but they seem to take in the scene in an instant. A slow smile pulls at their mouth. "Someone's been busy."

Sol's hiss sounds downright dangerous in a way I've never heard before. His crest flares wide. "Leave the things and get out."

If he talked to *me* like that, I would have fled for my life. Ramanu just leans against the doorframe. "Impossible. The balm you don't need me for." They pause meaningfully. "Though I'm more than happy to assist in applying it."

"Ramanu, *enough*."

Their grin widens. "But the translation spell? That's a trade secret. I'll need to get up close and personal with your little bride to give it to her."

The hissing sound gets deeper, almost like a giant rattlesnake.

I stare at Sol. It's like he's a completely different person. Distantly, I'm aware that this must be the *territorialness* he mentioned. I reach out but hesitate making contact. If he's this angry, he might strike out.

No.

I take a slow breath. If he's hiding a violent streak that might be leveled at me, better to know it now. I don't trust Ramanu, but they serve at Azazel's will, and *he* promised my safety. If Sol strikes at me, no doubt I'll be spirited away from him. It might not save my life, but *I have to know.*

I gently lay my hand against Sol's back.

The reaction is instantaneous. His crest lowers, and he moves back into my touch. The aggressive body language doesn't disappear, but he no longer seems in danger of attacking. I clear my throat. "Please, Sol. I would very much like to be able to enjoy your library." The words come out hoarse with fear, but there's not much I can do about that.

He half turns to look at me. "Very well. Ramanu, I suggest you work quickly."

"'Twas beauty tamed the beast," Ramanu mutters as they approach. They chuckle as if they've amused themselves and don't bother to skirt around Sol's still-bristling body. "This won't feel pleasant, but it will be relatively quick."

They sink onto the stool next to me and turn to face me, bracketing me in with their big thighs. Sol lets out another deep hiss and moves to stand at my back, close enough that I'm pressed against his chest, and he towers over us both. I'm rather closed in, but somehow, with Sol touching me, it's not enough to cause me to panic.

Ramanu pulls out several strange-looking tools and grins at Sol. "Now your bride will have *two* bargainer demon marks. How delightful."

"It's ill advised to provoke me, demon."

"So you say." They move quickly, using their claws to slash open their forearm.

I watch, frozen, as they dip one of the tools into their blood. Without asking, they swipe my robe off my shoulder, and it's only my body reacting on instinct that has me catching it in time to keep from exposing my breast. Sol lets out another hiss.

Ramanu, of course, ignores it and leans down, pressing the tip of the tool to my skin. It *hurts*. I wasn't awake for the first translation mark, so I can't speak to a comparison, but it feels like tiny teeth biting into my skin. I hold perfectly still, clamping my lips together to keep a whimper inside.

The demon keeps their attention on the dark red lines they're inking into my skin. I've only caught glimpses of the new tattoo on my back, but this is in the same style. One last swipe that has me biting down a scream, and Ramanu sits back. "Don't touch this while it heals. It will be fine by tonight. If you damage it and the spell doesn't work, that's not my responsibility."

"Get out," Sol rumbles.

Ramanu leans back slowly. "Don't let your *animal urges* harm your little bride, lizard. It would be such a shame for you to lose your territory because you can't control yourself." They push to their feet and pretend to consider. "On second thought, rip her to shreds."

Sol moves, a flash of green that appears in front of the demon. He grabs their neck and slams them back against the wall hard enough that I'm surprised the entire keep doesn't shudder.

"Sol, wait!" I start to rise, but the room goes strangely liquid.

I manage one step before my legs give out and everything goes dark.

CHAPTER 17

BRIAR

$\mathcal{I}$ come to before I hit the ground, Sol's arms around me. He lifts me just as carefully as he always seems to touch me when we're not having sex. The violence that screamed from his body language is gone. Or at least directed outward.

"Leave," he snarls.

"See you around."

I blink blearily at Ramanu as they walk out of the kitchen, apparently none the worse for Sol's attempted strangulation. Then they're gone and we're alone again. Strange how I used to see Sol as the threat, but now the tension goes out of my body with Ramanu's absence. They haven't done anything, but danger comes off them in waves despite their irreverent attitude.

Maybe my instincts aren't as fucked up as I believed.

"Briar?"

"I'm fine," I say automatically and then have to stop and ensure it's the truth. "I just got a little light-headed when I stood up."

Sol turns and sets me back on the stool, but he doesn't move away. "You passed out."

"I don't think so."

He exhales slowly. "You passed out," he repeats firmly. "Eat the rest of your food, and then I'm taking you back to bed."

My stomach is twisted in knots, and I'm not hungry anymore, but he's got an air about him that says he won't move from this spot until I eat at least a little more. I sigh. "Humans pass out from needles or pain all the time. It's nothing to be concerned about."

"I disagree."

He watches me closely, tension lining his shoulders, and I quickly take a few bites. "I'm fine."

"You keep saying that, but you'll forgive me if I don't believe you." He watches me eat for several long moments before taking a slow step back. "You would put your needs second to negating conflict."

I start to argue, but he's right. Best I can tell, he's been honest with me since I arrived here. It feels disingenuous to lie to his face in response. I swallow one last piece of fruit and sit back. "Old habits are hard to break. I've been here less than a week. I think I can be forgiven for not suddenly becoming a new person."

"I'm not asking you to. But you'll forgive *me* if I take steps to ensure you don't endanger yourself out of habit." He eyes the plate. "You're finished?"

"Yes."

Sol nods and makes short work of the remaining food, then he cleans and puts the plate away. When he returns to me, he seems even more serious than normal. "I mean it, Briar. I don't expect you to suddenly be without scars." He pauses.

I blink, still chewing on his earlier statement. "I'm not endangering myself."

"All the same."

I don't know what to say to that. The easy way we were before Ramanu came in is gone, replaced by tension. Sol is keeping himself tightly leashed, but there's no missing how tense he is. A frisson of something that isn't quite fear goes through me. "Would you have killed them?"

"Perhaps."

In that moment, I wish Sol were a little *less* honest. "You can't just go around murdering people who look at me sideways."

Instead of answering, Sol sweeps me into his arms. He pauses to grab the container Ramanu left on the counter, and then he's stalking back through the halls. They're eerily silent, which makes me realize they haven't been up to this point. "Sol?"

"You have nothing to fear from me."

I don't know if that means there's someone else in this keep that I should fear, or if there's someone in this keep that should fear *him*.

He carries me up to our bedroom and kicks the door shut behind us hard enough that, again, I'm glad this place is made of unshakeable stone. Sol stops in front of the bed and takes a long breath. It's only then that I note the slight tremors in his arms.

He hisses softly. "Do you trust me, Briar?"

With my heart? Most assuredly not. I'm not certain I even trust him with my future, since we are diametrically opposed in a number of ways. But he's not asking for either. I look up into his dark eyes. "What do you need from me?"

"I am..." He releases another hissing breath. "It's the mating frenzy. I didn't expect..."

Ah. I reach up and tentatively press my hand to his broad chest. "You need to reclaim what's yours."

"Yes."

I'm familiar enough with the concept of jealousy pushing someone to this kind of action, even if my past experience always made it feel like I'd somehow done something wrong. It doesn't feel like that with Sol. But then, nothing feels like I expect with Sol.

I drag in a breath. "I'm still very sore. You'll have to be careful."

"Trust me."

Just like that, it's an easy decision. I nod. "Okay."

Sol sets me on my feet and whisks off the robe. He's moving too fast for me to help, so I stand there and allow him to push me back onto the bed and guide my legs wide. He stands there for a long moment, staring at me almost as if he's about to say something, but then he blinks and the moment passes.

He strips out of his pants. God, his cocks are out and look even bigger in the late-morning light than they did last night. I can't stop the shaky breath as he stalks toward me, but he doesn't immediately cover me with his body.

He sinks onto the bed and wraps one giant hand around my thigh. Sol jerks me closer until I'm nearly in his lap and drags his tongue along my calf and presses my foot to his shoulder. The position leaves me obscenely open. I'm not quite so far gone as to do more than shake as he stares at my pussy. "Sol, I think—"

"I won't hurt you." His voice sounds different. His gaze doesn't move as he reaches with his free hand to the container Ramanu left. He lifts the lid with a practiced flick of his thumb, and a soothing scent fills the room. I don't recognize it, but it reminds me of the lotions and bath bombs that promise a "spa experience."

His claws *snick* away, and he dips one massive finger into the container. The scent gets stronger. I lift my head in time to see him press that finger into me. Sol swirls his finger idly inside me. It makes me flinch on instinct, but I quickly realize the soreness that's plagued me since we had sex is... gone? "What—"

"The balm isn't numbing." He gently saws his finger in and out of my pussy. "It's specifically formulated by the..." An angry hiss. "By *them*. It's healing you."

Them. The bargainer demons.

Sol withdraws his finger to scoop up a bit more of the balm, and this time, when he presses into me, he does it with two fingers. He watches himself fuck me with his fingers for several beats. I'm helpless to do anything but the same. It feels just as good as the first time he touched me like this. Better even, because he's already found the spot inside me that makes everything go a little hazy. "*Sol.*"

"You're mine, bride." He moves his hand from my thigh over my waist and up to bracket my ribs, pressing one breast up as if in offering. "My bride to do with as I please. I will fuck you until you can't take any more, then I will use the balm to heal you and do it again." The words are harsh, but his touch remains consistent, unraveling me at the seams. "Look at this pretty pussy. So fucking obedient. Wet and needy, just for me."

My back bows, but he holds me down. It only makes what he's doing between my thighs hotter. "Yes!"

"Ramanu would fuck you if you gave them half a chance." He gives that dangerous rattling sound. "They would spear you with their cock and fill up *my* pussy."

"No," I whisper. I shake my head hard against the bedding. "I wouldn't let them."

Sol lifts his gaze. "No, you wouldn't. Do you know why?"

I worry my bottom lip. I can barely move with him

holding me immobile, but I try to roll my hips to take his fingers deeper. "Because my pussy is yours." I sob out my breath. "*I'm* yours." In that moment, I almost believe it. Pleasure builds through me in ever-increasing waves.

Then Sol dips down, and his long tongue is at my clit. It's as if he has some magic that lets him know exactly where to touch, how hard, in what motion. Within seconds, I'm on the edge. "*Sol.*"

This time, he has no words for me. He's intent on my pleasure, and that focus tips me right into a back-bowing orgasm. I cry out so loud, I have the distant thought that I'll be embarrassed about it later.

He doesn't give me time to ease down like he did in the past. Instead, he withdraws just enough to flip me onto my stomach and urge my hips high. I almost tense up—it's such a vulnerable position with my cheek against the bedding and my ass in the air—but then his hands are wrapping around my thighs, his claws pricking skin so sensitive that the pain almost feels like pleasure. "There you are," he murmurs.

He feeds me one of his cocks a rough inch at a time. I thought he was impossibly deep last night, but it's nothing compared to this position. It feels like he's splitting me in two. He doesn't give me much time to adjust, but my body makes way for him. Just like it did last time.

I fist the sheets when he bottoms out inside me. My breath sobs from my lungs. I'm so full, I'm certain I can feel him in the back of my throat. "Sol, *please.*"

"Are you begging for mercy, bride?" He squeezes my ass cheeks, making me jump. "There is no mercy here." He withdraws just as smoothly as he entered me. I panic halfway through and try to shove back onto him, but he holds me immobile, continuing his retreat until just the head of his thick cock remains inside me.

"I like you like this. Shaking. Whimpering. Needing me."

He shifts behind me, one giant hand coming to rest beside my head as he bends over me. His breath is warm against my ear. "Beg, bride."

I try to slam back on him again, but he moves with me easily, somehow maintaining just the head of his cock inside me. I slap the bedding. "Sol, stop teasing me and *fuck me*."

I'm suddenly afraid he won't do it. That he'll keep teasing me until I lose my mind entirely. "Please, Sol. *Please fuck me.*" Words spill from my lips, fumbling words spill from my libs, need making them nearly incomprehensible. "Please don't make me wait. I need you."

His hiss rattles through his chest and into my back. Sol's claws dig into the bedding next to my face as he does exactly what I beg for. He picks up his pace, fucking me hard enough to draw gasps and whimpers from my lips.

Not hard enough to hurt me, though.

My orgasm takes me by surprise. One moment I'm trying to lift my hips, to take him deeper yet, and the next I'm cumming so hard, I scream. Sol pulls out of me and flips me onto my back. I blink up at him, dazed and drugged on pleasure. He presses my thighs wide, and I look down to see his top cock glistening with my orgasm.

Sol notches his bottom cock at my entrance and then looks at me. "I'm going to mark you, bride."

It's not a request, not really, but I nod all the same. "Do it."

CHAPTER 18

SOL

I'm going too hard, but I can't stop. Not after Ramanu's taunting, after seeing them mark Briar with their own blood. I hadn't realized bargainer demon tattoos functioned in such a way, and my lack of foresight bothers me just as much as everything else in the kitchen.

I need Briar to wear *my* mark.

It doesn't matter that she already is in the form of the little teeth marks patterning her lower stomach from when I fucked her with my tongue. It's not the same. I can't bite her. Not when I'm like this. I'm barely holding on to control, barely able to ensure I don't accidentally hurt her.

But there are other ways.

I push into her pussy. She gives one of those little mewling cries that make my entire body go tight. No matter what else is true, my little bride loves being fucked by me. I stop halfway inside her and grip her thighs. As much as I would love to penetrate her with both cocks, the reality is that it would do actual damage to her. So we'll improvise.

I hold her gaze as I spit, my saliva hitting my top cock and her pussy. She flinches but then gives a delicious little wiggle when I thrust deeper. "*Oh.*"

Oh, indeed.

I press her thighs together, trapping my upper cock against her clit. The fit isn't nearly as tight as her pussy, but it feels really fucking good. It feels even better when Briar cries out, "Oh god, Sol. Don't stop."

She might be almost timid other times, but when her pleasure is on the line, she's remarkably vocal. I love that. I switch my grip on her thighs to one hand and brace the other on the bed next to her. "You take my cocks so sweetly, bride." The words feel ripped from my chest. Watching her come apart around me is more intoxicating than any drink I've had. It *soothes* me knowing that she's coming on *my* cock, that she's begging *me* to fuck her deeper, harder, faster.

Mine.

Briar orgasms, clenching around my cock so hard that I don't have a choice about following her over the edge. I pump into her harder than I intend to, chasing my end. I release her legs, shoving them wide, and press my hand down against my upper cock, pinning it between us as I fuck her. "You're going to be a good girl and take my seed."

"*Yes!*"

I hiss as I fill her up just like I promised. As I *overfill* her, my seed cascading out of her around my cock. My top cock jerks, coating her stomach and breasts as I spurt onto her skin. Marking her.

It calms me further, but there's still an edge I can't quite remove. I ease out of her and retract my claws. "More."

"Sol..."

I swipe my finger through my seed and press it into her. "More," I repeat. I finger fuck my cum back into her slowly, letting her whimpers and cries soothe me further. This. This is what I need. *Who* I need. "Take it all, bride."

"I…" She gasps. "Oh fuck, I'm going to cum again."

I want to keep her like this always. Naked and spread for me, covered in *me*, her pussy overflowing with me even as she orgasms around my fingers again. Her entire body goes slack, her legs splaying out, boneless.

I almost keep going.

I want to.

In an attempt to regain control, I close my eyes, but it only makes the scent of our fucking stronger. Already my cocks are going hard again. *Fuck.* "I need to go."

"No."

I open my eyes as she fights her way into a sitting position and grabs my wrist. "Don't you dare."

I could break her hold easily, but *she's* reaching for *me*. It takes everything I have not to topple her back onto the bed and spear her again. "If you don't release me, you're going to get fucked again." I drag in a rough breath. "I'm not fully in control right now, Briar."

"Because of Ramanu."

I have her on her back in an instant. I stop short with my hand inches from her throat. "Do *not* say that demon's name in my bed." Fuck. What am I *doing*? I jerk my hand away from her vulnerable skin, but I can't quite make myself retreat.

Briar meets my gaze boldly. There is no fear in her eyes, which doesn't make any sense. I'm not in control right now. It's never been like this with anyone else. I don't know what I might do. I can't guarantee anything. It scares me, so how can it not scare her? The last thing I want is to make her think I'm like *him*.

She licks her lips. "They're not in bed with me, Sol. *You* are." She drags her hands down my chest and then back up again. She grabs my wrist and guides my hand to her throat. The only warning I get is a reckless look in her dark eyes before she snaps my leash. "But if you leave, maybe I'll see if they're still around."

I black out for a second.

One moment I'm staring down in her with shock and rage. The next, I have her on her stomach, and I'm shoving my cock into her pussy. Too rough. Too fucking rough. But I can't stop. "I'm going to fuck you so hard, you'll be too sore to even think about another cock."

"Do it," she taunts. "If you think you can."

I slam into her again. It's not enough. If she can still talk, then I'm not doing my job properly. I squeeze her ass cheeks, parting them and staring down at her tight little hole. She can't take one of my cocks there, not when I'm barely in control and unable to prime her correctly... but there are other options. "You *will* be full up with me."

I use my tail to grab the small bottle of oil from the dresser next to the bed. She's so small, it won't require much. Just enough to ease the way. She squirms when I dribble oil between her cheeks.

"What—*oh fuck.*"

I press the tip of my tail into her. She spasms around my cock, but I hold her steady. "Take it, bride." Just a bit more, just enough to fill her up. I stare at the pretty sight of my tail in her ass and my cock in her pussy. "Yes. This."

I reach down and grab her hand, guiding it between her thighs to where my second cock is. "Hold me tight to you."

"I can't..." She squirms, making my vision short out. "What are you *doing* to me?"

I could ask her the same thing if I had the words for it. I need to be deeper, to fill her more, to have that pretty pussy fluttering around my cock as she cums again. *For me.* I start moving, quickly finding a rhythm that has her making those delicious pleasure noises. I don't need to fuck her with my tail, not when it's adding to the fullness of my cock in her pussy. More, I don't know what she can take and as much as part of me wants to fuck her until she passes out, there's enough reason left to caution against it.

"You are *mine*, Briar Rose." I rut her like a mindless beast, each word dragged from my chest in a voice I hardly recognize as my own. "My pussy that I will fuck as long as hard as I want. My tight little ass." I lean down and hook her throat, bending her back so I can taste her tongue. "My mouth to play with as I see fit."

She presses my cock harder to her clit, shivering and shaking around me. She can't speak with my tongue in her mouth, but she doesn't have to. I can feel the resistance in her. I don't know if it's play or not. I'm not certain I care. I shove deep enough to make her squeak. I have to break the kiss to keep speaking. "If you touch another, I'll rip their throats out, and then I'll fuck you in the pool of their blood. *Do you understand me?*"

"Yes," she sobs.

This time, when she cums, I manage to hold out, to slow down enough to not follow her to the very end. I don't let up, though. The tide of rage is receding, will be gone with the next orgasm, but part of me wants to cling to it a little longer. Right now, she's not drawing lines in the sand between us. She's limp and pliable and oh so wet with the combination of us.

My orgasm is coming on too intensely to deny. I pull out of her at the last moment and come across her ass in great spurts. Almost... I shove my second cock into her, and only then do I start fucking her ass with my tail, working my seed into her there as well.

My second orgasm bottoms out inside her and takes the last of my strength. I slump to the side and haul her with me to sprawl across my chest. We're both sticky with bodily fluids, which I find strangely soothing.

Mine.

I don't realize I've spoken aloud until she says, "Yes, you've made that abundantly clear." I tense, expecting a well-deserved snarl or two. Now that the mating frenzy is easing, it's clear I went too far. Again.

But Briar nuzzles my chest and wiggles until I wrap my arms around her. She lets out a soft sigh. "I'm going to need more of that balm."

"I'm sorry."

She lifts her head. She looks a mess. Her red hair is tangled, and there are tear tracks on her face. But the smile she gives me is sweet and a little sinful. "Don't be sorry, Sol." She reaches up and cups my jaw with her hand. "I just came so many times, I lost count. There is absolutely nothing to apologize for."

It feels good to have her in my arms like this. *Right.* I had every intention of utilizing every resource available to bring her around, but this strange feeling in my chest is happening too quickly, too strongly. I'm free falling, which I want to enjoy, but I can't quite relax enough to do so.

Most of my people lost the ability to fly centuries ago.

I can't shake the suspicion that I'm setting myself for a brutal landing that will leave me bloody and broken when this is all over.

CHAPTER 19

BRIAR

W e don't make it to the library for two more days. I can't say I'm complaining. Our time is spent alternating between outstanding, filthy sex and softer moments where he takes care of me. Sol keeps watching me as if he expects me to crumple, but the second things start to heat up, his control snaps, and he's wringing every bit of pleasure from my body possible.

Even so, I can't shake the frisson of glee when I wake up and find him already dressed. He looks down at me, his eyes going hot, but he gives himself a sharp shake. "I promised you the library, Briar. Get dressed and we'll go down."

He got a bit creative with the healing balm last night, so I'm only vaguely achy as I climb to my feet and duck into the bathroom. Fifteen minutes later, I'm as ready as I'm going to be. Sol makes a move like he's going to carry me but aborts it halfway through.

As much as I like being carried by him—and I do—it *is* rather nice to walk through the halls side by side. Sol matches his longer stride to mine, and the silence is perfectly comfortable. As we descend the stairs, I realize I've stopped watching him closely, waiting for some indication he's hiding a true monster inside.

I won't change my mind about having a child only to leave them behind, but I can't deny that Sol seems to be a genuinely good person. He's kind and caring and completely willing to play bedroom games with me without any judgment or shame. I'm still trying to wrap my head around it.

Sol goes still, his crest rising the slightest bit as he sees who waits for us at the bottom of the stairs. "Aldis."

She's wearing what I've come to realize is customary dragon clothing. Her pants are a deep blue that contrasts her scales beautifully, and they swish about her legs and tail almost like a skirt. They're much fancier than the plain—if luxurious—ones Sol seems to prefer. Her vest is a matching blue and, unlike how Sol wears his, she's buttoned it up to cover her breasts. She looks lovely.

For her part, Aldis doesn't even look at me.

I would take it as a slight but for the careful body language she's conveying and the aggression wafting off Sol in waves. This is his cousin, but he's treating her almost like how he dealt with Ramanu.

She bows slightly. "You're two days behind on correspondence."

Just like that, his crest deflates and his shoulders slump. "The others do realize I'm the one who runs this territory and, as a result, they should be fine waiting for me to reply at my leisure, correct?" The words *should* sound arrogant and brash but instead come out almost hopeful.

Aldis shakes her head. "You know that isn't how it works."

"Yes, I suppose I do." He sighs. "Can I bother you to bring it into the library? I'll wade through the paperwork there."

"Of course." She sketches out another bow. "Breakfast, as well?"

"If it's not too much trouble."

She makes a distinctly amused sound. "I'm more than willing to help out for now." Aldis risks a glance at me, her dark eyes warm. "You look well, Briar."

"I am, thank you."

She turns on her heel to stride away from us before Sol can do more than hiss a bit. As soon as she turns the corner, his crest lowers completely. I eye him. "Mating frenzy, huh?"

"I can't control it entirely right now." He shakes himself. "It will get better with time."

We head down the hall and into the library. I can't help the little sigh of happiness at being in this space again. Most of the rooms in the keep are rather comfortable, but this one feels downright magical.

I take a step toward the stacks of books and stop short. "Is there anything in here I shouldn't be handling?"

"Anything dangerous is locked up in our vault. Nothing here can hurt you."

I was more asking about what *I* might damage, but I suppose that's answer enough. I start forward, only to be brought up short when Sol hooks an arm around my waist. "Food first."

"But—"

"I have a feeling I'm about to lose you for hours." His voice is warm and indulgent and makes me feel strangely soft. "Food first, and then you can explore until lunch."

I'm tempted to argue just to see what he'll do, but it's a fair ask, and truth be told, I *am* hungry. I turn in his arm and smile up at him. "Thank you. You didn't have to ask Azazel to send Ramanu to tattoo me. I know you didn't like it."

"It had nothing to do with them spelling you and everything to do with them poking me until I wanted to bite their head off, horns and all."

I'm not entirely certain he's joking. In fact, I'm suddenly sure he's doing that brutal honesty thing again. I should *not* find the idea of Sol biting someone's head off in my defense charming, but I'm having a hard time keeping perspective. This realm is so different than the one I was born to. It seems brutal in some ways, but I've been met with more kindness in a short week than in all my life.

Azazel, strangely protective of his contracted humans.

Sol, so big and ferocious and gentle at the same time.

Even Ramanu. They're aggravating in the extreme, but how long would Sol and I have avoided each other if they didn't intervene?

Aldis appears with a plate of food, and Sol and I chat easily as we make quick work of it. It's all small talk, which is partly my fault, because I keep shooting looks at the books. He finally sits back with a hissing laugh. "Go, Briar. Have fun exploring."

I rise. I have every intention of hurrying to the stacks, but I impulsively throw myself into his arms. *"Thank you."*

Sol hugs me close for a long moment and then sets me on my feet. "All you have to do is ask. If it's within my power, it's yours."

An extravagant promise. He is the ruler of an entire territory, and while I might not fully understand how large that might be or what it entails, it doesn't change the fact I could abuse this promise. There's an element of trust in the offer. I'm not certain I deserve it.

I smile, my throat tight. "I'll keep that in mind."

Entering the stacks feels like entering yet another world. It's even quieter than the rest of the keep, and the soft sound of my dress swishing about my legs feels almost absurdly loud. I pick a book at random, a thick leather-bound tome. It's heavy enough that I sink to the ground to open it, and I hold my breath as I do. Will Ramanu's spell work?

The words give a sickening swirl and then reform before my eyes into English. I run my fingers over the ink wonderingly. Magic. Strange how I can encounter so much beyond comprehension, but *this* is the magic that has my heart filling with wonder.

The book, it turns out, is a textbook on the anatomy of a kraken and how it's evolved with the introduction of humans to the bloodlines. I flip through a few pages, mildly curious, before I close the book and carefully slide it back into its place. It wasn't a kraken who won me in the auction.

I'm more interested in dragons.

The sheer number of books quickly overwhelms me, so when I find what appears to be a children's storybook section, I grab a stack of the books and haul them back to the main sitting area.

There, I find Sol wading through a stack of paperwork nearly as tall as he is. I blink at the thick vellum scrolls and sheaves. "What's all this?"

"Correspondence." He hisses with displeasure. "Harvest reports, which are slightly less upsetting." Sol glances at me. "They're very curious about you. Once things...ease...we'll have to entertain."

Things being this mating frenzy that makes him so aggressive. I worry my bottom lip. "Will things change with *us* when that eases?"

He gives me a long look. "No."

I set my books on the low table between us, careful not to disrupt the papers. I kind of want to sit next to him, but surely that's not necessary? We might be married, but we're hardly...

"What are you doing, Briar?"

I stop in the middle of inching toward the empty couch. "Sitting down?"

He cocks his head to the side and studies me. I don't know what my expression is doing, but Sol eventually says, "Would you like to sit with me?"

It's on the tip of my tongue to lie. After everything we've done, I don't know why *this* feels too intimate. But when I open my mouth, the truth emerges. "Yes."

Sol shifts over, though the couch is plenty large enough for both of us. It's obviously made for two dragons to sit on, with plenty of pillows instead of two larger back cushions like I'm used to. I feel like a child burrowing into them, arranging them around me in a little nest for maximum reading comfort. After I'm settled, Sol relaxes back and slides his tail partially around me.

I pick up the first book and settle down to read, though I'm achingly aware of how close he is. He watches me for a few seconds and then almost reluctantly turns back to his stack of *correspondence* and reports.

The book is fascinating. It doesn't quite follow the same story structure that I'm used to, feeling more like a poem than a story, but a lot of older human stories were passed around in poem form, so I suppose that's not so unfamiliar. What *is* familiar is that it's a teaching story the same way so many children's books seem to be.

I work through three of the books while Sol dramatically decreases his pile. Aldis appears at regular intervals to whisk away the completed work.

It's...cozy.

I've never done this before, this casual sharing of space with no expectations and no tension. Growing up, my parents were of the mind that if one person is cleaning or working or doing something, then everyone needs to be doing it as well. And my mother was *always* cleaning. It wasn't until later, when I found myself in my own unhappy marriage, that I realized she used it as a kind of escape. It wasn't enough of an escape for me.

I frown down at my book, the words no longer comprehensible through no fault of the spell. "Sol?"

"Hmm?"

I frown harder. "What am I supposed to *do?*"

He finally looks at me, appearing to give me all his attention. "What do you mean?"

"I can't do this all day." I motion at myself, reclining and comfy and far too relaxed. *Lazy,* an insidious voice whispers in the back of my mind. *If you don't prove your worth, he'll know you're really worthless.*

Sol hesitates. "Do you want to do something else?" He glances at the paperwork. "I really should get this done today, but if you want, we can spend some time outside the keep tomorrow."

"That's not what I mean." I close my book and struggle to sit up, the cushions hampering the movement until he wraps his tail around my waist and helps. I shiver. "Am I supposed to spend seven years just lazing about?"

His attention narrows on me. "You've been here a week, Briar."

"Yes, but—"

His tail flexes around my waist. "When was the last day you spent in leisure without worrying about *lazing about?*"

Heat flushes through me, and I can't tell if it's embarrassment or shame or something infinitely more complicated. "That's not the point."

"I would like you to answer the question."

I really, truly don't want to. I see where he's going with this, and he might be right, but it feels like he cracked open my ribs and is staring at my still-beating heart. Too vulnerable. Too honest. I can't hold his gaze. "I don't remember."

"Briar." He gives me another gentle squeeze with his tail and catches my chin between his claws, guiding me to look at him again. "There is no shame in taking time for leisure. In giving yourself space to find your feet."

It's too good to be true. He's saying this now, but surely

he'll start to resent me as time goes on. Unless he truly does see me as a pretty pet to be kept. The thought leaves me cold, but I can't tell if it's because the fear is unfounded or not. "I like having a purpose."

Now is where Sol will tell me that my purpose is bouncing on his cocks. Or remind me I'm only here because he wants me to bear his child. *Something* to snap me back into reality and remind me this isn't some lovely fantasy without teeth.

He finally releases my chin and sits back. "Very well. What would you like to do?"

That's the thing.

I don't actually know.

CHAPTER 20

BRIAR

J don't have an answer for Sol that day or the ones that follow, one week bleeding into another. He doesn't pressure me, but sometimes I catch him watching me as if he expects me to shatter...or explode.

I keep myself occupied in the library. I could spend an entire lifetime digging through the stacks and still not make it through them all, but that's not a bad problem to have. They keep me occupied. Distracted. Mostly engaged.

It would be lovely to say that being with him whisks away all the bad bits of my past, but it's not the truth. I still have nightmares. I still jump every time a door slams or I hear unfamiliar footsteps.

Yesterday, I broke a plate and nearly cut my hands in a panicked flurry to clean it up, apologizing all the while. There was no one even in the room to apologize to. No one even noticed that the kitchen was missing a plate, or at least neither Sol nor Aldis brought it up.

At night, well, I love the nights. Sol and I fuck like each time might be our last, as if he can feel the seconds slipping through our fingers just as quickly as I can. Seven years felt like a small eternity, but as I reach the one-month anniversary of my marriage to Sol, I can't shake the feeling that it's nowhere near enough.

Seven years. Only eighty-four months.

Eighty-three now.

"Briar."

I blink and blush. "Sorry, I was just thinking."

Sol swirls his wine in his goblet. I know him well enough now to read his expressions most of the time, and he's got a contemplative look I'm not certain I like. He's very careful with me—that hasn't changed in the past month—but I can tell something's bothering him. He finally sits back. "Are you happy here?"

"What? Why wouldn't I be happy?" Maybe I shouldn't be. Even as pleasant as I find Sol's company, it doesn't change the fact this is an impossible situation with a deadline. We are at odds in purpose, even if we're not at odds in anything else.

He doesn't answer. He merely waits. I kind of hate it when he does that. He never allows me to divert a question with a question when there's something he really wants to know the answer to. Or that he feels I need to share the answer to. It's inconvenient, but no matter how frustrating I occasionally find this habit, I can't pretend it's done out of anything except caring for me.

I take a hasty sip of my wine. "Yes. I'm happy here." It's even the truth. He was right that day in the library. There's something healing about having nothing but time to spend as I choose. To spend it with *him* in a comfortable way that makes no demands. He hasn't brought up the child again, though *filling me up* plays into many of our sexual encounters.

I shiver and take another sip of wine. "I still don't have an answer to your question. I don't know what I want, Sol.

Maybe this would be easier if I did." He's mentioned a few times that his late parents co-ruled together, but it feels like a huge imposition to the dragon people to attempt to do that when I have no intention of staying.

Sol considers me. "Let's get out of here tomorrow. At least for a little bit."

It's something we've been talking about for weeks, but something always seems to come up and put off the plans. I smile. "What about the newest batch of reports that came in this morning?"

He hisses a little. "They can hold for a day. I'd like to show you the land beyond the keep."

A thrill goes through me. I haven't left the keep since the first day I arrived. Thankfully, the mating frenzy has eased enough that Sol doesn't mind Aldis spending time in the library with us during the day, and I've really enjoyed her company. But he's not comfortable bringing more of his people back into the keep yet. Not when every time Ramanu arrives for their weekly check-ins, they rile Sol up so much, he spends the rest of the day and night fucking me damn near unconscious and covering me with his seed. It might be vaguely worrisome if it didn't get me off so hard. Maybe it's worrisome that it *does* get me off so hard. I'm not an innocent bystander; I find myself taunting him in those moments, spilling words to make his frenzy spike and his control snap.

Reckless of me, perhaps, but he's never given me cause to regret it. Truthfully, he's admitted that it turns him on just as much as it turns me on. Bedroom games. I never knew they could be so much *fun*.

Still, my reading has brought plenty of things to my attention about the land surrounding this place. "What about the predators in the forest around here?"

He gives what amounts to a toothy dragon smile. "I'm the most dangerous predator around."

I laugh. "I believe it." I sip my wine. "I would like to see some more of your territory, Sol."

"Good."

* * *

THE NEXT DAY dawns bright and clear as if Sol controlled the weather to create a perfect environment. I almost went with pants today, but Sol told me we weren't going particularly far, and I like how he looks at me when I wear dresses.

He leads me out a different exit than last time, heading in the opposite direction from the holy spring. Now that I'm not dazed and almost in shock, I take in the forest we move through with interest. I'm hardly an outdoorsy person. These trees look like...trees. Large enough to defy belief, but I couldn't begin to say if they're different than the ones in my world. They must be. The food I've been eating is all vaguely familiar and yet strange at the same time, as if maybe the food I'm used to and the stuff here had a shared ancestor at some point but evolved in wildly different directions.

For his part, Sol walks beside me in comfortable silence. It's always comfortable. He doesn't feel the need to fill the space between us with words unless he has something to say. It took me nearly a week before I stopped jumping every time he shifted, certain he'd require my attention.

He seems happy just to be in my presence. It's...nice. Especially since I feel the same way. I find spending time with him incredibly soothing—at least when we aren't having sex. There's nothing soothing about *that*.

"What are you laughing about over there?"

I trail my fingers down his arm and then lace them with his. "Just thinking that sex with you is anything but restful."

He snorts. "I would hope not. The only time you're

tempted to sleep in the midst is when I've fucked you unconscious."

"That was *one time*." And not even truly unconscious. My body just stopped working, overloaded with pleasure and sensation. "And it wouldn't have happened at all if I didn't feel safe with you."

His hand tightens around mine, the tiniest of flexes. "I don't take that for granted, you know. That you feel safe with me."

My chest gives a slightly horrifying flutter. I swallow hard. "I know."

A month of peace isn't enough to fully distance myself from nearly half my life spent afraid. I wish it was. I wish I could wave a magic wand and eliminate all my scars, but that's not how life works. I can't unlearn half a lifetime's worth of habits in a single month, but I'm no longer waiting for the other shoe to drop with Sol.

I'm...happy.

Sol leads the way off the main path and up a narrower dirty trail that has me huffing and puffing. Strangely, I relish the effort. The air tastes different out here. I don't know how to explain it. The keep is always kept cool and comfortable and feels slightly icy on my tongue. This is almost the exact opposite. The air is faintly humid with a weight I can feel against my skin. If it were much hotter, it would be irritating, but it's pleasant in this moment.

We reach the crest of the hill, and Sol steps out of the way, revealing a paradise. The trees are spaced farther apart up here, their thick canopy parted to let the sun in uninterrupted. A meadow of white and blue and yellow flowers leads to a small lake that backs up against a higher cliff. It looks like something out of a painting.

"I spent a lot of time here as a child." Sol lifts his head and closes his eyes as the sun paints his face.

We've talked about our childhoods a bit, but only in broad terms. We're both only children, which I've found to be a bit of a sore spot for each of us in different ways. I'm sure there are plenty of people who have no siblings and were perfectly happy, but with my parents the way they were, it was an incredibly lonely childhood. From the comments Sol has made, I think his was the same. His parents loved him dearly, but they had many responsibilities that kept them busy.

"Why didn't your parents have more children?"

He looks down at me. "They tried. There was a time when my people would have families with large numbers of children, but it hasn't been that way in generations."

I worry my bottom lip as we start for the lake. "Is it like that with all the territories in this realm?"

"Only the kraken. The rest haven't had the same difficulties we have."

Easy enough to read between the lines there. I don't understand how humans and dragons were able to breed in the first place, but it obviously acted as more than a conduit for magic. With each generation without humans mixed in, the difficulties rose.

Guilt clamps around my throat, but I try to swallow past it. I am one person. I cannot solve the entirety of this territory's problems.

You could solve some.

I shove the little voice away. I like Sol quite a bit. Possibly more than like. In another life, I would have bent over backward to give him anything he wanted, anything he needed. I'd like to think that I wouldn't give him a child I had no intention of sticking around to raise, but I can't say for certain. Desperate times call for desperate measures, and survival was my only rule for so long.

I *can't* do this.

If this didn't end in seven years...

But that thought hurts worse than the others. With what I've discovered about Azazel and the bargainer demons' hold on the power supply in this realm, I can't imagine he'll let me stay past my end date.

More, for all that Sol seems to enjoy my company and my bed, he never signed on for a permanent human wife. The only reason we're married at all is so any child—the *true* goal of this contract—will be legitimate. If his plan went to perfection, I would leave him with a child and a wide-open spot for some nice dragon person to fill. Not his ex—he mentioned that they are married to someone else now—but he fell in love enough to consider marriage before. Surely he will after I'm gone.

"Briar." From Sol's tone, this isn't the first time he's said my name.

"Sorry, I was just thinking." I turn to the gorgeous scene in front of me. Maybe the lake will ease my worries.

Except there's nothing to be worried about. There's no gray area, no unknown outcome. The path is beneath our feet, and it only leads to one place. I just didn't expect to dread the future deadline instead of welcome it.

"Do you swim?"

I blink up at Sol. "What?"

"Do you swim?" he repeats patiently. He's always so damn patient. He never gets mad at me when I mentally wander and am not entirely focused on him. He simply tugs me back to the present if he needs my attention...or lets me wander if he doesn't.

I look at the lake again. I'd only intended to walk along the pebble beach and get my feet wet. "I know how, but I'm not the strongest swimmer." I haven't had much cause for practice, even if the bathtub here is nearly large enough to count as a pool.

"You don't have to join me, but do you mind if I do?" He rubs a hand over his head. "It's been a long time since I've been up here, and it's my usual method of working through challenging problems. I think better when I'm swimming."

"Go ahead." I watch with avid interest as he strips out of his pants and vest and walks into the water. I don't know what I expect, but I'm strangely delighted to discover he swims similar to how a crocodile does, spearing through the water nose first in sinuous movements. It's enthralling even as some deep prey instinct shivers in response.

I hug my knees to my chest and watch him as the sun climbs in the sky and the balmy air starts to feel sticky. I can spend hours and days and weeks worrying about the future...or I can enjoy the time I have now.

The future will come regardless of what I do.

The feeling in my chest feels a bit like sorrow and yet somehow more bittersweet. It's not going away anytime soon. Maybe not ever. But Sol is right here, right now.

I push to my feet and start to undo my dress.

CHAPTER 21

SOL

The past month has been downright blissful. It's so *easy* being around Briar that the mating frenzy would have passed entirely by this point if not for one single friction point that continues to rile me.

She's holding herself back.

It's nothing more than I expected, but she gives her body and her time so freely, I resent her withholding her heart. I know she's worried about the future, about the past. Truthfully, I'm worried, too, albeit not for the same reasons. This woman has worked her way under my skin in a few short weeks.

She's intelligent and has a charming tendency to blurt out whatever she's thinking and then look mortified immediately afterward. She's also so incredibly *brave*. Even after everything she's gone through, she's still striving toward the light. It leaves me in awe. She meets me halfway in the bedroom and then some, seeming to enjoy the possessive mating frenzy as much as I've begun to. She riles me up and then welcomes me with open arms.

I've never met another person like her. I don't know that I ever will again.

It's not even the possibility of no children that bothers me. No matter what I told her during that first week, I'm in no rush to breed. Dragons might not live as long as we used to in generations past, our lifespans much closer to humans and topping out at one hundred and fifty except in rare cases. It's not an eternity, but we have time and plenty of it.

Except we don't.

Seven years seemed rather excessive when Azazel first offered the possibility of a human bride. I fully intended to enjoy her and then, eventually, enjoy raising the inevitable children once she'd returned where she'd come from. I dive deep beneath the water, but the icy depths of the lake do nothing to calm the racing of my mind.

Now? I'm not certain I won't rip out Azazel's throat if he tries to take Briar from me.

As I swim upward, I catch sight of Briar moving into the water. I pick up speed. I should have warned her that I have more than enough lung capacity to stay below for quite some time. I should have realized she might worry if I went down and didn't come back up, but sometimes with our differences, it feels like fumbling around in the dark. I don't know what I might stumble over until I'm on my knees.

I surface some distance away in an effort not to startle her, and the small smile she gives me is just an intoxicating as the sight of her nude body framed by water as she wades deeper. She's gained weight since arriving here, and it pleases me greatly to see that her bones no longer jut out against her skin. She's softer, and I hope that means she's happier as well.

The water hits her ribs, and she shivers. "It's colder than I thought."

"It's barely summer. It won't get much warmer than this,

though." I swim slowly toward her. "You changed your mind."

"I think too much." She reaches out, and I don't hesitate to take her hand and drag her through the water and into my arms. It's deep enough here to reach my shoulders, which means it would be well over her head. Briar wraps her legs around me as best she can. "Do you worry about the future with us?"

I'm not often tempted to lie, but I don't know what she's been mulling over. There's a right answer to this question and I want to give it to her. But maybe the right answer is simply being honest. "Yes."

She traces my jaw with her fingertips. "I didn't expect it to feel this complicated, especially in such a short time."

Again, honesty wins out. "Neither did I."

I want to keep you.

It's not a fair ask. My feelings might be getting softer and yet more intense at the same time, but after everything she's gone through, I refuse to be another person in her life who tries to tie her down and shear away parts of her so she can be mine in perpetuity. She only bargained seven years. She hasn't said anything to suggest she wants longer, and with our current positions, I can't be the one to broach that subject.

And after a month? She'll laugh in my face.

Except she's Briar, so she won't. She'll just get quiet and withdrawn, and I'll lose her years before she walks out of my life. It's not a problem that will likely have an answer at all, let alone today.

Instead, I can give her some good memories.

"Swim with me."

She immediately tightens her grip on me. "When I said I wasn't a strong swimmer, I meant the last time I swam was like twenty years ago." She peers through the crystal-clear

143

water to where the ground drops out a few feet beyond us. "I think I might be afraid of deep water."

"I won't let you go under." I carefully pluck her off me and bracket her waist with my hands. "And there's nothing to be afraid of in this lake. My family has been coming here for generations, so even when there's gaps in our visiting the space, the predators know better than to try to move in."

"Predators," she squeaks.

"Do you remember what I said before?"

Briar looks up at me with those big dark eyes. "That you're the biggest predator around."

"Yes." It's the truth, though the reasoning isn't quite as simple as I've suggested. The reason there aren't overly dangerous predators in the area surrounding the keep is because we kill any that come too close. Over the years, most of the packs learned to leave a large swathe of territory to us, and in turn, we leave them be. Dragons are predators in their own right, but a pack of kelpie could take down an adult, not to mention a child.

I have a feeling telling Briar that explicitly will frighten her. She might be an adult, but she's human. She has no scales or claws or teeth to defend herself. The thought leaves me cold even as a surge of protectiveness goes through me. "I won't let anything hurt you."

She looks at me for a long moment and then finally nods. "Okay. What do I do?"

It's a strange experience teaching a human what dragons seem to know instinctively. Her body isn't shaped like mine. She can't swim the same way I do. I end up bracing a hand across her torso just below her breasts and holding her afloat as she tests out movements to see what works best. Briar is clever, and once she sets her mind to something, I've noticed that very little deters her from the pursuit of that outcome.

Swimming is no different.

Within an hour, she's bobbing about, paddling and laughing in a carefree way that feels like she reached out and hooked me in the chest. She swims into my arms and climbs my body to press a kiss to my snout. "Thank you for today, Sol. I think I needed this."

Stay with me.

Again, I don't say it.

But, as I follow Briar back to the shore, I finally recognize the feeling that's been taking root in my chest, tendril by tendril. *Love*. The realization makes me both buoyant and feels like someone strapped a weight to my chest and tossed me off a cliff. It was different with Anika. I loved them, could picture the rest of my life with them, but when my parents ended the courtship, my heartbreak only lasted a few months. Because I didn't lose Anika. Not really. We're still friends. They're still in my life.

When I lose Briar, she'll be gone without a trace. I'll never see her again.

Briar wades out of the water, stopping long enough to ring out her bright hair. She shoots me a look over her shoulder, and her brows draw together. "What's wrong?" she asks in my language.

She's been doing that a lot more lately. Trying out draconian in small sentences as she gets more comfortable with our lessons. Her mouth really isn't made for it, but she's more than coherent, and every time I hear it on her tongue, I get a little distracted.

Figuring out how to circumvent the translation spell wasn't as simple as I would have liked. We had to ask Ramanu—Azazel—for help. They practically gloated to have more of their blood tattooed into Briar's skin, but the end result was worth it. Briar can turn off the translation spell for our lessons. Or whenever she wants, really.

I clear my throat. "Nothing."

"Sol…" She hesitates. "You just lied to me."

It's entirely too tempting to dive back beneath the water and just swim until I run out of breath. I'm…afraid. I give myself a shake and hold her gaze. "You're right, I did." I exhale harshly. "But I would rather not talk about it."

Briar searches my expression for a long moment and then finally nods. "Okay." She moves toward where her dress is and tugs it over her head. I start to worry that I've upset her, but she turns to me with a soft smile. "If you change your mind, I'm here."

"I appreciate the offer." Does she realize how novel it is that she doesn't press? It's on the tip of my tongue to tell her everything, to confess what I'm feeling, but I hold it back at the last moment. It's not fair to put that on her. It doesn't matter what I'm feeling now, and it certainly doesn't matter how that feeling will inevitably grow as time goes on.

"Sol."

Something's different in Briar's voice. I refocus on her to find her cheeks turning a charming pink. "Yes?"

"On the day that we met." She won't quite look me in the eye, her fingers twisting in her hair almost frenetically. "Do you remember what you said to me?"

I said a lot of things to her that day, but I'm not certain what she's thinking of specifically. I hold perfectly still, watching her closely. "Remind me."

"You said." She sucks in a breath that makes her breasts bounce. Briar finally lifts her chin and holds my gaze. "You said if I ran, you'd chase me."

Heat surges through me, but I force my legs still. "I remember now."

Briar takes a small step back, and I can't stop the instinct that has me tensing to pursue. She smiles a little. "Chase me, Sol." Then she takes off into the trees.

CHAPTER 22

BRIAR

$\mathcal{I}$ haven't thought beyond giving Sol something to think about other than whatever is bothering him. Sol's threat from the first day we met has plagued me, making my skin feel too tight and my pussy throb with need. I haven't had the courage to ask for this kind of game before now. As I crash through leaves nearly as long as I am tall, I wonder if I've made a mistake.

I can't hear him pursuing me.

Maybe he was so shocked by the suggestion that he's still standing by the lake, staring after me. Should I go back? Or…

Even as the doubt tries to creep in, a deep roar sounds from somewhere behind me. It reminds me of a show I watched a long time ago where some lord sent his hunting dogs after a woman. They'd howled kind of like that, except this is a thousand times more powerful. It triggers every prey instinct I have.

Suddenly, this is no longer a game.

I'm running for my life.

I pick up speed, ducking between the leaves and flying across the ground. It's not exactly kind to bare feet, but I barely feel the scratches. Fear bites at my heels, bringing with it a breathless kind of exhilaration. Is this what skydivers feel when they see the ground rushing up to meet them?

Sounds behind me. Something large is crashing through the trees in my wake. I let out a little shriek and run faster. In my time in the keep, I've learned that Sol is all but silent when he moves, a true predator who's accidentally snuck up on me. After doing so the first time sent me into a full panic attack, he's very careful to ensure I always hear him coming or have some auditory warning that he's near me.

He's not trying to be quiet right now.

I look around frantically. Maybe I can climb—

A weight hits me from behind. Another shriek bursts from me as Sol takes me to the ground, creating a cage with his larger body. This should be the end of it, but that fear-exhilaration has me by the throat, and I'm acting purely on instinct. As he rolls, I squirm out of his arms and try to scramble to my feet.

Only for him to wrap a massive hand around my ankle and jerk me back to the ground. I keep trying to get away, my fingers clawing at the dirt, as he drags me backward to him. It causes my dress to rise around my thighs.

We both freeze when the fabric hits my hips. The pause barely lasts a beat of my racing heart, and then Sol wrenches me closer and surges up to cover me with his body. I try to shove him off, but it's impossible.

I love that it's impossible.

He flips me onto my back and catches my hands in one of his own, forcing them over my head. I get a look at his face for the first time since I laid this gauntlet at his feet and took off running. Sol looks...feral. There is no logic or reason in his eyes as he digs his claws into my dress and rips it open from the thighs down.

I've lost more than a few dresses to Sol's claws in the past few weeks. I know he can divest me of the thing in a single swipe. He's doing it slowly now on purpose. My entire body breaks out in goose bumps, and I struggle harder. Even I'm not sure if it's in earnest or simply because the feeling of him holding me down makes me so turned on, I can't think straight.

Another rip, and I'm bared from the hips. The force of the next rip jerks my body from the dirt. The fabric of my dress parts around me, leaving me naked beneath Sol's predatory gaze. It doesn't matter that I was just naked with him in the lake or that he watched me pull this dress on after we swam.

It feels different.

My breath is fire in my chest, my breasts heaving from panting. Sol is breathing hard too, his hot exhales ghosting against my nipples. Even so, I hear the near-silent *snick* of his claws detracting the moment before he pushes *two* fingers into me.

"Fuck!" My back bows so hard, my breasts actually brush his mouth.

Sol strikes.

His jaws close around my throat.

I freeze, torn between true terror and a pleasure so fierce, it makes me dizzy. He works me with his fingers even as his teeth prick my skin. My body can't decide if I'm going to cum or start screaming and never stop. The sensation of his hot breath against my skin only gets more intense as his tongue flicks against the hollow of my throat.

He presses his thumb to my clit and starts to fuck me with his fingers; long, slow slides that have pleasure building inside me in steady waves. I blink up at the forest canopy, my fingers grasping at nothing from where they splay over his grip on my wrists.

"I can't…"

He twists his wrist, and that's all it takes. I orgasm with a scream that seems to shake the very trees around us. Or maybe it's simply *me* who's undone completely.

Sol withdraws his mouth, his teeth dragging lightly across my skin. They catch my pendant, pulling the cord taut. It stretches out between us. But he doesn't snap it. Instead, he holds perfectly still.

Waiting for me to tell him no.

I *should*.

But the game has me in its clutches, and I can't do anything but stare in silent challenge. I can't tell him yes... but I won't tell him no, either. Sol hisses and then jerks back. The pendant snaps and flings off into the distance.

We stare at each other for several beats. Then Sol moves back onto his knees, jerking his fingers from me and gripping me about the waist. He uses one arm around my waist to lift me into the air upside down. My legs fall open in surprise, and then his mouth is on me, teeth once against pressing to my skin as his tongue delves into my pussy.

I cry out and writhe. Every time he does this, it unravels me entirely. I'm fighting it this time, but all the fight does it remind me how little control I have. He's still got my wrists pinned together against one thigh, and with my hair hanging in a curtain around my head, I'm all but cut off from the greater world.

If he doesn't stop, I'm going to cum again.

I look down to his two cocks, which are so hard, they seem painful. Sol chooses that moment to make his tongue roll inside me, seeking my G-spot. *Oh god.* That will never, ever get old. I writhe harder, and Sol bends a little, just enough that I can reach his cocks with my mouth. He's far too big to take, but that doesn't stop me from licking and nipping at him in a frenzy. In response, he only seems more intent to make me cum all over his face.

If I just had my hands...

But it's hotter that I don't. That he's holding me immobile. That I'm having to fight to reach as much of his cocks as possible. That he keeps fucking me with his tongue even as his teeth create little pinpricks of pain against my lower stomach and ass.

He eases his tongue out of me and presses it to my clit, pulsing there even as I sob. "Sol, *please*." It's too much and not enough, and I'm shivering on the brink.

He doesn't leave me there. He never does. Sol strokes me just how I need to send me hurtling into an orgasm that curls my toes. On and on it goes until the finally gentles his touches and lowers me to the ground.

I blink up at him, dazed and punch drunk off pleasure. Now's the moment when he'll fuck me. The thought thrills me down to my very bones. I have very carefully colored within the lines for my entire life. Only since I've been with Sol have I started to understand that there's nothing forbidden when the people involved are on the same page.

This has higher consequences that anything you've ever done.

I don't care.

I don't want to stop.

Except Sol is easing back. His gaze is still downright feral, but he's holding himself restrained in a way I recognize from that first day, and again the first time we had sex. If left to his own devices, he won't give either of us what we want out of a desire not to push me.

He's probably right. In fact, I *know* he's right.

That doesn't stop me from wobbling to my feet and taking a staggering step back from him. Sol tenses, his claws digging into the ground. "If you run," he grinds out. "If you run, bride, I'm going to fuck you right here in the dirt."

Desire thrills through me so intensely, I weave on my feet. I hold his gaze and take another step back, and then another.

He's creating deep furrows in the ground, obviously thinking I'm trying to ease away from him.

I turn and run.

Or at least I try. My legs still aren't working properly and so I manage three stumbling steps before Sol takes me to the ground. This time he doesn't give me a chance to brace. He loops an arm beneath my hips, lifting them as he shoves one cock into me. I shriek. My body has learned the shape of him, but usually he gives me more time to adjust to his size.

Not today.

His jaws close around the spot where my shoulder meets my neck, and he lifts my hips higher until my knees leave the ground. I'm wrapped up in him again, helpless to do anything but take his cock as he slams into me. I try to scramble, my toes digging into the dirt, but it's no use.

So I stop fighting. It feels too good to keep it up. Instead, I reach down and press my hands to his upper cock, creating a delicious friction for both of us between my hands and body. In response, Sol hisses against my skin and fucks me harder. He fills me to the point of near pain, but my wires have long since been crossed for whatever we do together. I shudder in his arms, the coming orgasm even stronger than the first two. "Sol!"

Put a baby in me.

The shame of even *thinking* that makes this whole thing hotter. I don't want that. I truly don't. But the threat of it only makes me wetter.

Sol loses his battle first. He surges into me and, god, I love this moment more than anything else we do. I *feel* him cumming, his cock swelling inside me, his seed filling me and then overfilling me, bursting out to drip down my thighs. "More!"

Sol jerks out of me and then arranges me on his second cock. We should stop, but the damage is already done. "Fill me up." I moan. "Please, Sol. Fill me up and make me cum again."

Three strokes are all I take to lose it. I cum so hard, every muscle in my body locks up painfully. Sol jerks inside me, filling me a second time. Only then does he unclench his jaw and slump back with me in his lap. His cock twitches inside me, and I writhe, which makes him curse. "Enough."

"I can't..." He lifts me off him, drawing a whimper from my lips.

Sol wraps his arms around me, almost too tight, and holds me to him. I cling to his grasp as our bodies cool and our heartbeats return to normal. His seed is still dripping from me, a distinct reminder of the risk we just took.

The risk *I* just took.

After all, Sol wants a child. That's the whole reason I'm here to begin with.

"Briar."

I close my eyes. I don't want his apologies, but I'm not ready to face the potential consequences for what we just did. I chose this, but that doesn't mean I'm not filled with a conflicting swirl of regret and desire. "I would rather not talk about it."

Sol's silent for a beat, and then two. Finally, he says, "Did I hurt you?"

"No." It's not quite the truth. My pussy is one big throbbing ache, though it's not entirely unpleasant. I'm also bleeding in various places from his bites, though as I look down, they're just little rivulets from the pinprick points of his teeth. I should *not* find the sight sexy, but there's little logic in how I am with Sol. "I'm fine."

"Liar." He rises slowly to his feet but doesn't set me down. "I'm carrying you back. Do *not* argue with me." There's something simmering in his tone, something deep and almost angry. I can't tell if it's directed at me or not, and when I look up at his face, I'm still unsure.

It's a fight not to hunch into myself, to make my body a smaller target. Rationally I *know* he won't hurt me, but some instincts aren't so easy to reroute. Sol's never been angry with *me* before.

I think I've just fucked up.

CHAPTER 23

SOL

I don't bother to go back to the lake to collect my pants. There's no one to witness this angry trip through the forest back to the keep. We're alone, me and my quivering bride. I can taste her fear on my tongue, and it makes me crazed. My instincts are still in the driver's seat, demanding I mark her, protect her, *breed* her.

I should have known that chasing Briar would mean I'd lose control. There wasn't a single thought in my head except catching her, biting off that damn pendant, and then fucking her until she admitted she was mine in every way that matters.

Two out of three feels like a hollow victory.

I should speak, should find the words to put her at ease. I have none. I want to promise her that if she'd told me to stop, I wouldn't have snapped off that pendant and tossed it away. I want to tell her that I wouldn't have fucked her without that protection if she hadn't run from me a second time.

I want to…but I'm not certain it's the truth.

For the first time in a long time, I wish my parents were still alive to give me advice. They had me late in life and

155

passed from this world together in peace a few years ago. After over forty years with them, I thought they'd taught me everything I'd need. I made my peace with missing them, but that's a normal part of moving into adulthood.

We dragons don't live forever, after all.

But I don't know what this is. I hardly recognize myself right now. My arms shake around Briar, and as I stride away from the trees toward the keep, I'm not certain if it's to deposit her in our bedroom and get some distance...or to lock us in together until she stops withholding herself from me.

No. Goddess, *no*.

She chose what we just did, for better or worse. She might hate me for it once the endorphins wear off completely, but she's too fair to blame me when it took both of us to get there. At least, I think she is.

Then again, I'm hardly thinking clearly at the moment.

"Sol."

"No." I shake my head and shove through the front door. "Not yet."

Briar curls tighter against my chest. "Okay."

We don't see a soul on the trip to our bedroom. It's just as well; I'm not certain what I'd do with this current mood riding me. I *hate* this. I don't lose control. I definitely don't misstep because of impulsiveness. And I sure as fuck wouldn't knowingly do something to put Briar in danger.

Even from me.

Except that isn't the truth, is it? Even as my surface thoughts say one thing, there's a deep part of me that's satisfied with the outcome of today. That loves the blended scents of our fucking. That's soothed by the sight of my teeth marks on Briar's skin.

I step into our bedroom and kick the door shut. "You will allow me to bathe and heal you."

"Okay." She sounds meeker than she ever has, a tremor in her voice that makes me want to hiss in rage. Except I can't because I'm the one who put it there.

I close my eyes and strive to sound more normal. I'm only partially successful. "You have nothing to fear from me."

"I know." The tremor is still there, but she sounds certain. "Truly, I do."

That certainty eases me enough that I'm able to walk into the bathroom and set her down. I keep one hand on her waist, ready to catch her if her knees buckle, but she manages to keep her feet. The tub is tempting, but we're both so covered in dirt that the shower is the better option. I turn on the water with one hand and then, as soon as it's warm, wash her.

There are already bruises darkening her skin in a number of places, and several of my teeth marks are still bleeding. But, by the time I finish, she's not shaking anymore. I wash quickly, hating the way my hands shake. It's not worry. I'm barely holding back the need to be inside her again.

This is so *wrong*.

I turn off the water and wrap Briar in the fluffy towel she confessed to loving in her second week here. She starts to protest that she can walk, but the words die as I scoop her into my arms again. I lay Briar on the bed and push her thighs wide. She watches me with an unreadable expression as I reach for the healing balm. "You don't have to do that."

"Yes, I do." I can't stop myself from watching her face as I scoop up some of the balm and press it into her. She looks like she wants to keep her eyes open, but as I concentrate on coating the inside of her pussy with the balm, she lets her head fall back. Her lips part in pleasure.

It would be so easy to keep this up. I know how to make her feel good. When we're fucking, she's not thinking.

It's the wrong thing to do.

Reluctantly, I finish applying the balm and ease my fingers out of her. Now's the time to have a conversation, to talk through what just happened, but I can't shake the fear that doing so means losing her. She's already made her thoughts on pregnancy with me clear. I had no right to remove that pendant, and we both know it. Another pendant will ensure she doesn't get pregnant from this encounter. But only if I hurry.

I shove to my feet. "Rest. I'll be back."

"Sol—"

I don't remain to hear whatever she's about to say. I might deserve whatever recriminations she sends my way, but at least if I replace her pendant, there's a chance of seeing this through. Of making it right.

I charge down the stairs and practically rip off my study door. The sheer force startles me, and I concentrate on slowing down, on not upending my desk to find the scroll I use to communicate with Azazel.

There's no reason to panic. I haven't lost her. She's right upstairs, and in a very short time, I'll have made this right and we can go back to how we have been.

My writing is horrid, but I manage to scrawl out my request.

There was an incident. I need another pendant. Immediately.

I stare at the scroll, waiting for the reply. It never takes long. I'm still not certain if Azazel himself does it or if he has someone on staff in charge of this kind of communication. It doesn't matter.

There is no response.

The seconds tick by into minutes. What the fuck is keeping him? I pick up the quill to write a second message when a shadow falls over my desk.

"What are you doing, Sol?"

I jump and then curse myself for jumping. Briar has taken

the time to wrap herself up in the blanket she seems to favor the most when I'm not readily available to keep her warm. Is that a sign she doesn't want me to come to her?

I'm spiraling. I don't know if I've ever spiraled before. No matter what trials arose, there has always been a logical solution. Even with Anika, my disappointment and heartache never overrode my ability to think. Right now, I'm not thinking. I'm panicking. I have to fix this, and I don't know how to. "Go back to bed."

"No, I don't think I will." She hitches the blanket higher around her shoulders and sinks into the chair across from me. "What's going on? Why are you acting so strange?"

"I'm not."

Her brows draw together. "That's the second time you've lied to me today." Her hand goes to her bare neck. "This is about the pendant, isn't it? Because you ripped it off."

"I'm sorry," I grind out. "I shouldn't have."

If anything, she frowns harder. "I'm sorry, were you the only person participating in what we did?"

Shame makes me hunch my shoulders. "That's not the point." I had never been more aware of the differences between us than when I stalked her through the forest. It *felt* like predator and prey, and I enjoyed it far too much. We weren't equals. "Ripping off your pendant and then fucking you was taking the game too far."

"You did *what?*"

We both startle as Azazel himself appears. He fills up the doorway, his horns curving up to scrape against the mantle as he steps into the room. His dark gaze takes us in, and his brows slam down. "Explain yourself."

"I—"

"Not you, Briar." He doesn't look away from me. "I want the dragon to explain why he's apologizing for *an incident* removing your birth control and then fucking you."

Apologizing to Briar is one thing. Putting what just happened out there for Azazel to sit in judgment is something else altogether. "That's between us."

"That's where you're wrong, my boy." He takes another step forward, looming over the desk. "My contract says otherwise."

Alarm bells peal through my head. Surely he doesn't mean to... I push slowly to my feet. "If I violated the contract, you would have been waiting here for me when we arrived back at the keep. You would have known before showing up that it happened."

He narrows his eyes. "The contract might not have pinged what happened as harm, but what I just heard *does*."

He's right and I hate that he's right. That doesn't mean I'm about to bend on this. Not when the stakes are so high. "We're fine. Leave."

"Briar." His tone is significantly softer when speaking to her than it is with me. "Did you consent to have Sol's children?"

She pales, her skin turning almost green. "What? No. I mean..." Her voice goes raspy. "We haven't talked about it since our initial conversation."

Azazel's dark eyes glimmer red. "And during that conversation, you told him you..."

She goes even greener. "That I didn't want children during this contract."

"Wait—" I'm not sure what argument I have, but in the end, it makes no difference.

His eyes flare crimson. "I don't know how one qualifies harm in *this* territory, but in *mine*, the definition clearly applies." He looks around. "I'll return to iron out the details shortly."

Briar looks between us. "Wait, that's not what I meant."

"Don't try to protect him now." He stalks to her, two

quick steps. I register his intent and dive for them, but it's too late. Azazel grasps Briar's shoulder and they blip out of existence, teleporting away from me.

Forever.

"No!"

CHAPTER 24

BRIAR

*O*ne moment I'm staring into Sol's panicked face,
watching him dive for me, and the next my stomach
gives a sickening lurch and I'm back in the room where this
all started. Or, rather, where my entrance to the demon
realm began. It looks almost alien after getting used to my
low bed and cluttered cabinets in Sol's room. I want to rip
the pretty lace curtains from the walls.

I jerk out of Azazel's grasp, well aware that he allows it.
"You're wrong!"

"I'm not." He eyes me, the red in his eyes retreating until
they're the more familiar black. It's not a heated look by any
means, but I am suddenly aware of the fact that I'm naked
beneath my blanket. Azazel frowns when I tuck it tighter
around myself. "Are you in need of medical care?"

I flush from my toes to roots. The only pain points are the
little teeth marks across my body, but I'll be damned before I
let him take those away. "I'm fine."

He nods slowly. "You're safe here."

"I was *safe* with Sol." I might have complicated feelings
about what happened and how he acted afterward, but I have

no doubt we were both victims to our lusts and a game going too far. He didn't set out intending to trap me. I certainly didn't set out to force him to violate the terms of the contract.

Azazel stalks to the wardrobe and flings it open. He grabs a robe and tosses it onto the bed. "Put this on, and then we'll get you another pendant. I'm assuming it hasn't been long since he tore the other."

"A few hours, maybe." I'm honestly not sure. I was pretty out of it after we had sex, and then I waited for more than a few minutes for Sol to come back to the bedroom before outrage gave me the strength to go hunt him down. For all the good it did me; our argument gave Azazel the ammunition he needs to call the contract into question.

Azazel moves to the door, presenting me with his back. "Time is of the essence. The pendant can prevent pregnancy as long as the process hasn't reached a certain point."

I blink at his back. "It's a magical Plan B."

"Something to that extent." He glances at me and frowns. "The robe, Briar."

I want to disobey out of sheer fury, but the fact remains that this must be the first step in digging Sol and I out of this mess. "I will come with you, but then you will *listen* to me."

He sighs and turns back to face the door. "Very well."

I drop the blanket and pull on the robe. It's a thick material that is soft and warm, and after belting it at my waist, it covers me even better than the blanket did. "I'm ready."

Azazel opens the door and allows me to precede him into the hall. It's a different hall than last time; my door is no longer at a dead end but now stretches a great distance in either direction. He turns right and leaves me to follow.

I curse him silently the entire time. Each step causes my anger to rise. I forget that Azazel is a *demon*, that he's nearly as large as Sol, that he is very much responsible for my being a widow the first time around. We turn a corner, and my fury bubbles right out of my lips in the form of a screech. "It's none of your business!"

The demon turns to me with an exasperated mutter that the translation spell doesn't quite convert. "You are under my care. Your safety is my responsibility."

I catch movement out of the corner of my eye, but I'm too focused on Azazel to care if we have an audience or not. "You're a nosy-ass demon who needs to let two adults have a conversation without you sweeping in and *kidnapping me*."

"I didn't kidnap you!" he roars.

I should be scared. I should be peeing my pants right now because not only am I in the middle of a confrontation, but it's with someone who could disembowel me with one swipe of his black claws. Instead, I'm roaring right back at him. "Your ridiculous contract didn't get triggered by what happened between us and you know it! I did not agree to come back here with you! I was having a *discussion* with my *husband*, not your high-handed demon ass!"

Azazel snarls in my face. His features haven't shifted, but they seem less human-like all of a sudden. "Get your ass in that room right now, and secure a replacement pendant. I'll deal with you when you're reasonable again. Calm down."

Everything goes staticky and strange. It almost feels like the top of my head explodes. Surely that's the only explanation for me launching myself at Azazel, fingers curled like claws. "You *bastard!*"

I never make contact.

Arms hook around my waist, jerking me back against a broad chest. I don't stop to wonder who grabbed me. I am not thinking about anything but ripping Azazel's horns right off his head and beating him to death with them. "Take me back! Take me back right fucking now!"

"That's about enough of that," a familiar voice says.

Ramanu.

They toss me over their shoulder. "I've got this covered, Azazel. It didn't require your direct interference."

"Take care of it," Azazel snaps. Heavy footsteps stalk away from us, but I can't see anything except Ramanu's round ass in my face.

"Put me down!"

"I don't think I will." They take a few steps, and then we're leaving the hallway and entering through a door I'm nearly certain wasn't there a few seconds ago.

I try to still my racing heart, determined to burst for the door the second Ramanu sets me down. There was a way through this place to Sol's keep before. Surely it still exists. I just need to find it. It will mean evading Ramanu and Azazel, but I don't care. I will *not* let things end with Sol.

Not like this.

Not without even getting a chance to say goodbye.

Ramanu drops me, none too gently, into a chair. They're there with a hand when I try to pop to my feet. I slam into their palm and drop back into the chair with a curse. "Let me go!"

"I know how little humans like to be told to calm down." They root around in a cabinet with one hand while the majority of their attention seems to be on me. "But the fact remains that I'm not letting you out of this room until you can walk nicely without trying to assault our leader."

"I wouldn't have to assault anyone if he didn't transport me out of Sol's study without so much as a question of whether I wanted to go."

Ramanu shrugs. "He holds your contract. He can do whatever he pleases, barring harm." They yank a pendant from the cabinet, identical to the one Sol ripped off me earlier today. "Hand."

I glare but finally thrust out my hand. They prick my

palm with a claw and press the pendant there, closing my fingers around it. The familiar jolt through my body makes me shake a little. I stare down at the pendant, my emotions a tangled mess.

I don't want to be pregnant. Not if it means leaving the child behind.

But... If I didn't have to leave? If Sol and I had a future without an expiration date? That's a different story altogether. I reluctantly drop the pendant around my neck and look up at Ramanu. My heart is still racing, my brain fuzzy, but I manage to speak without screaming at them. "Please take me back to Sol."

"That's not my call to make."

"And yet you managed to make all sorts of calls while you've been checking in on me over the past month." I cross my arms over my chest and glare. "You know damn well that Sol would cut off his arm before he'd ever actually hurt me. He hesitated before he ripped the other pendant off. He also hesitated before fucking me. *I ran.* I knew what would happen if I did, and I did it anyways. If anyone's caused harm in this scenario, it's *me.*"

I knew he was having regrets, that he was feeling guilty for what happened. If I hadn't hesitated to go down and talk to him because I knew the conversation would be uncomfortable, we wouldn't be in this mess. We could have spoken and figured things out without Azazel appearing to set the whole damn contract on fire.

Ramanu sighs. "You have to understand, little bride. Azazel might be the leader through sheer might and viciousness, but he's an overprotective daddy bear when it comes to his precious contracts. Regardless of your intent, he's only seeing the bottom line. He's not thinking any more clearly than *you* are right now. Give him some time to cool down and then explain things. I doubt he'll change his mind, but you have a better chance of getting him to listen than screaming at him in the hallway."

What they're saying makes sense.

I don't care.

I rise slowly to my feet, daring them to intervene. "Either tell me where Azazel will have gone, or take me back to Sol."

"I told him this was a mistake. The other leaders are too damn stubborn, and humans are nothing but trouble."

I don't think Ramanu intends for me to hear that, so I ignore it. "Fine. I'll find a way myself."

"Patience."

Yeah, I don't think so. I'm not feeling patient in the least. The second they turn for the cabinet, I head for the door. If Ramanu won't help me, then I'll just figure this out for myself.

I make it one step out into the hall when something sharp pricks my neck. My legs go out, and Ramanu scoops me into their arms as my bones turn to jelly and an overwhelming numbness spreads through me. "What..." My lips won't move properly.

"If you won't have patience on your own, then I'm forced to *persuade* you. Sleep tight, little bride."

CHAPTER 25

SOL

It takes three days to reach the bargainer demon territory. Normally, it would take five, but fear for Briar has me ignoring my body's exhaustion as I hurry to reach her. I barely stopped to pack supplies before I went after her, wouldn't have thought to do so if Aldis hadn't waylaid me before I reached the front door.

If Azazel sent her back...

What will I do?

What can I possibly do?

No one stops me as I cross the territory line. I can hear the demons just out of sight, can sense their presence as they shadow my path to Azazel's castle. He's chosen to allow me to approach, and I can't begin to say if that's a good thing or a bad thing. I'm not thinking clearly, and I know it.

It's too late to worry about it now.

I charge up the steps to the castle. Again, no one stops me. This is becoming absurd. I throw open the door to find the grand entrance gone, replaced by a featureless hallway leading to a single door. "Subtle."

The door opens into a study that isn't dissimilar to mine.

There are shelves of Azazel's personal book collection, a large desk stacked high with enough paperwork to give me pause, and a demon waiting for me behind it.

"Shut the door." Azazel's eyes are a glowing crimson. "If you start roaring, I will kick you out of here so fast, you might not survive the portal out."

It's tempting to flip this desk the same way I flipped the one in the keep. My own office is destroyed, and no doubt once I've calmed down, I'll feel a deep shame about that. It feels like I've been acting on instinct since meeting Briar, and it's caused no end of missteps. "Is Briar okay?"

Azazel raises his brows and sits back. "That little hellcat nearly took my face off."

I stop short. "What?"

"You heard me."

"I did, but…" But at no point during my acquaintance with Briar would I call her a *hellcat*. Those beasts haunt Rusalka's territory, and even *I* would hesitate to go up against one. Briar can be impulsive at times, and I refuse to think about what we get up to in bedroom games while in the presence of Azazel, but she's nowhere near the ferocity of a hellcat. "You've made a mistake."

"That's what she keeps saying." Azazel presses his claws to his temples. "Sit down."

I don't want to. I shouldn't have energy after making the trip here in such a condensed timeline, but the fact remains that I'm fighting not to pace about the study. I reluctantly sink onto the backless chair sitting in front of the desk. "I understand I signed a particular contract with you, but I didn't realize you were so interested in expanding the bargainer demon territory."

Azazel stares at me for a long moment, expression unreadable. "You have something to say. Say it."

"I had some time to think while traveling." Without Briar

to focus on, several things became rather clear. "Several years ago, you said you wanted peace between the territories. I didn't believe you. None of us did."

He doesn't move. "I fail to see what influence your belief —or lack thereof—has to do with me or our current circumstances."

I ignore that. "It made sense that you'd set up a spiderweb with four neat little traps that will put you in charge of the entire realm. I didn't question it." I lean forward. "But you don't want my territory, do you? You don't want any of ours."

Azazel holds my gaze for a long moment. "You wouldn't believe the gift without the strings attached. So I made them hefty ones." He shrugs. "Even if I took all four territories, I wouldn't hold them indefinitely. Your respective peoples are too powerful and too stubborn. It's more trouble than it's worth."

I'd begun to suspect as much, but the confirmation leaves me a bit rudderless. "Then why take Briar?"

"*That*, I was not fucking around with." Just like that, his relative ease is gone, replaced by menace. "I realize the rest of you think we keep the humans here as our playthings and see them as little more than toys to be used and discarded when the deals are up. That's not how it works. A contract is sacred."

Something akin to guilt flares. He's right. I thought the worst of him and his people. Worse in some ways, I utilized their presence for my own pleasure while thinking that. "I owe you an apology."

"I truly couldn't care less what you think of me." He leans forward, matching my posture. "But you harmed one of mine, and *that* I will not forgive."

"Briar is not *yours*. She's *my* wife."

"Your wife *by my leave*."

The door swings open behind me, and I leap out of my

chair, fully expecting an attack. Except it's not an assassin slipping through the door. It's Briar. She's more put together than the last time I saw her, her hair pulled back into a complicated twist and wearing a deep-gray dress that looks absolutely devastating on her.

She catches sight of me and stops short. "Sol?"

I have so much to say, it all gets tangled in my throat. The only thing that emerges is her name. "Briar."

She starts to move toward me, but Azazel flings out a hand. "I swear to the Goddess, if you throw yourself into his arms right now, I will send you back to the human realm."

I hiss, but the sound dies in my throat as Briar spins on him. She gives a truly impressive snarl. "You're so high-handed, it's no wonder Eve doesn't want you!"

Azazel, leader of the bargainer demon territory, *flinches*.

Far from being deterred by landing an obvious hint, Briar strides to the desk and plants her hands on it, sending two mounds of paperwork cascading to the floor. I wince in sympathy before I remember I'm as furious at Azazel as she is.

"You're out of line," he rumbles.

"I'm not the only one." She leans forward, showing not an ounce of fear. "Am I pregnant, Azazel?"

His expression goes flat. "That's irrelevant."

"It is not irrelevant, and you know it, or you wouldn't be dodging the question. Am. I. Pregnant?"

He leans back and crosses his arms over his chest. Not a vast retreat, but a retreat nonetheless. "You know you're not. I can smell your cycle from here."

"Do *not* sniff her," I hiss.

Briar ignores me. "Your entire argument was that Sol caused potential harm by removing my pendant even though your damned contract didn't think so and neither did Sol nor I. Since said pendant is now back in place and I

171

am most assuredly not pregnant, by your logic, no harm was done."

He glares. "I liked it better when you were frothing at the mouth and trying to attack me."

"I'm glad we're in agreement." She straightens. "With that in mind, how does the end of the contract work?"

Now Azazel's watching her just as closely as I am. "Should I allow you back with the dragon—and that's a rather large *if*—then at the end of seven years, I will collect you." He hesitates, clearly not wanting to continue, but under Briar's glare, he relents. "And then I would offer you a choice to return to your realm or stay in mine."

I must make some sound of shock, because he glances at me. "It's customary, even if we don't advertise it. The majority of bargainers return to their realm to enjoy whatever it is that they gave seven years for. Only a small percentage stay."

Briar takes a small step back from the desk. "Thank you for answering. Since we're in agreement, I'm returning with Sol."

Azazel shakes his head slowly, a small smile pulling at the edges of his lips. "You're a terror."

"Thank you," she says primly. "In the future, should I need your assistance, I will call."

He raises his brows and looks at me. "I take it I'm being dismissed."

Unlike Briar's new confidence, I'm not certain this will end the way I hope. I nod slowly. "I would like to take my wife home." A weighted pause. "With your leave."

For a moment, I think he might deny us simply to do it, but he finally waves at the door. "Take your hellcat and leave."

I can hardly believe it. I thought for certain I'd be walking into an all-out fight to get Briar back...and not necessarily one I'd win. The cost was more than worth it. Now, Azazel is allowing me to walk out with Briar, an expression on his face that's somehow both indulgent and exasperated.

For her part, Briar tucks herself against my side. She shoots Azazel a vaguely apologetic look. "I'm sorry for what I said about Eve. I'm sure you two will figure things out."

I swear smoke actually comes out of his nostrils. "Leave."

We leave.

Ramanu waits outside the door, that smirking smile firmly entrenched on their face. For once, I don't want to rip their head right off their body. They motion to a door that wasn't there when I arrived. "Might as well make the trip home an easier one."

I don't argue. The only thing I care about is getting Briar home and then talking through things. I don't have more clarity about *that* even if the time apart gave me other angles to look at when it comes to Azazel.

The last thing I want to do is hurt Briar, but she's also made it clear she won't allow me to shoulder the full guilt for our misstep. I don't know where that leaves us. I'm a bit afraid to ask, but we can't move forward until we work through this.

I truly hope her fury at the demon means she wants to move forward with me.

We step through the door and into the familiar halls of the keep. Briar tilts her head back and inhales deeply. "I missed this. I thought I'd never be able to come back here."

"Briar—"

She opens her eyes. "We need to talk."

CHAPTER 26

BRIAR

J had a lot of time to think over the past three days, especially after Ramanu tossed me in with Eve, the woman Azazel chose for the auction. I am not the same person who made that demon deal a month ago. A *month?* It feels like a lifetime. That woman never would have dared go toe to toe with Azazel several times over the past few days.

The woman I was would be able to look into the future and see a life without Sol by her side. She might not have been overly eager to return to the human realm, but she had no intention of staying.

I don't feel that way anymore.

Sol leads me to the library, and I allow him to pester me into wrapping up with a large blanket and drinking some hot tea. Truth be told, now that the excitement is mostly over, I feel like napping for about twelve hours, curled in a ball while I wait for the worst of the cramps to pass. A little bit of fussing from Sol actually does make me feel better.

Especially when he sinks onto the couch next to me and drapes his arm over my shoulders. I snuggle up to his side, careful not to spill the tea. "Are you stalling?"

"Maybe a little." He nuzzles my temple. "I'm sorry things got out of hand. Azazel might be a bit of a prick, but he wasn't wrong."

"Sol." I sigh. "I was there, too. I didn't tell you to stop." I take a quick swallow of the near-scalding tea. "I got off harder knowing we shouldn't be doing it. It took two of us to get into that mess. Please stop trying to shoulder all the responsibility."

He tenses like he wants to argue but finally hisses a bit. "It won't happen again. I promise."

It's so tempting to read into that for the worst possible explanation—that he doesn't want me to stay—but that interpretation doesn't make sense. If Sol didn't want me here, he wouldn't have chased me all the way into a different territory. He wouldn't be worried about harming me at all.

Communication isn't easy. I've never had to be particularly good at it, other than reading the room to anticipate and respond to the undercurrents. This is different. This isn't about protecting myself. This is about what my heart wants...if I'm courageous enough to reach out and take it.

I swallow hard. "It's only been a month."

"I know."

"I'm still working through so much. I might spend the rest of my life working through it. I'm a mess."

His arm tightens around me the finest bit. "You're not a mess, Briar. You're a survivor."

A survivor. I never understood how powerful that term could be until now. Not a victim. Not broken. A little banged up and a little fragile, but a survivor, nonetheless. I lean forward to set down the mug and twist to face him. From the beginning, Sol has taken his cues from me. Even when he's hissing and pressing me on certain subjects, he always responds to my mood and comfort level.

I want to give him the same gift.

I clear my throat. "I know you want a child."

"Not if it means I lose you." He shakes his head sharply. "I'll find another way to help my people. You're not a pawn, Briar. I'm sorry I saw you as one to begin with."

"Sol." I glare. "Will you let me finish?"

He has the grace to look sheepish, his head bowed and shoulders hunched. "Of course. Please continue."

It would be so much easier to just let him lead. But if I truly want this, then I can't take a back seat for the entirety of the future. I don't *want* that. "I..." God, why is this so hard? "I love you, Sol. I don't know what the future will bring, but there's nothing for me in the human realm. If you want...If you're interested..."

"I love you, too." He presses a claw to my chin, lifting my face to his. "Stay with me, Briar. Forever."

I go dizzy at the sensation like my heart is expanding until it's too big for my chest. "Truly?"

"Truly." He presses his forehead to mine. "And if you never want children, that's—"

"I do," I blurt. "Not yet. I need to work through some things before I'm willing to bring a life into this world. And, well, I'd like to enjoy some more time with only you. But I do want children eventually."

Sol exhales slowly. "Then, when you're ready, we'll figure that out. Together."

Together.

"Okay," I say slowly. I wait for him to retreat enough that I can once again see his face. "But what about this mating frenzy? We can't spend the rest of our lives locked up in here away from everyone else."

Sol drags a hand over his head. "It will ease. Truthfully, under normal circumstances, it would have already done so. I... I think that knowing you want to stay will help. Before, every second passing felt like grains of sand slipping through my fingers. I didn't want to share that precious time with anyone." His crest rises and falls. "Give me a week, and we'll see where we're at."

Progress. I'm sure dragons are as varied as humans are, so there will be bumps along the way. Regardless of how common humans might have been in the various territories in the past, they aren't common now. "Will they accept me? I don't know if I'm qualified to be a co-leader, but I want to be a full partner to you, no matter what that looks like. Maybe I can work with Aldis and help with the paperwork."

"She would love that. *I* would love that." Sol, being Sol, doesn't give me a pat answer. He gives me an honest one. "Some of my people won't accept you. There are a small number who firmly believe we never should have bred with humans, but those dragons tend to keep to themselves and prefer their own company. They don't come to the keep often, if at all." He shrugs. "The rest fall on a spectrum of personal and political beliefs. Some will try to get close to you in order to bend me to their agenda. Some will be curious. Some might react in ways we can't anticipate." He narrows his attention on me. "Does that bother you?"

I honestly don't know. The thought of being exposed to that many people, to have some relative form of power and need to avoid missteps... It's a lot. "I'm going to mess this up."

He brushes back the few strands of hair that have escaped my updo. "Missteps happen, because we are not perfect creatures, but I'll be here, and Aldis will be here, and there will be others. You're not alone, Briar. The territory and its people do not hang in the balance on you being a perfect queen." He hisses a little in amusement. "And if Azazel has his way, there will be lasting peace between all the territories, which will only lower the stakes involved."

I frown. "You think we were peace offerings."

"I think Azazel is playing a deeper game than any of us know."

I consider the woman I met while in the demon's tender care. He might have an agenda for the greater realm, but I have a feeling whatever is going on with Eve is significantly more personal. I *do* feel a bit bad for throwing her in his face earlier, but he's a big demon; he'll get over it.

"You're likely right. But he's not our concern right now." I snuggle closer to Sol and wrap my arms around him as best I can. "Tell me again."

He pulls me into his lap. "I love you, Briar.

"I don't think I'll ever get tired of hearing that."

"I'll never get tired of telling you."

I hug him tight. "I love you, too, Sol. I never thought I'd end up in an actual fairy tale with my very own dragon Prince Charming, but I wouldn't have it any other way."

EPILOGUE

BRIAR

I used to think happily ever afters only came in storybooks. In real life, your Prince Charming is much more likely to hide secrets of a Bluebeard variety than actually be a paragon of virtue.

The past five years have proven otherwise, and I've never been so happy to be wrong. I press my hand to my round stomach and carefully pick my way along the park after Sol. He's offered to carry me no less than four times, but despite it nearly being time to meet our baby, I'm more than up for the walk. It feels good to stretch my legs.

It feels even better to return to the place that started it all. Or at least started it all between me and Sol.

He reaches the clearing and waits for me to catch up, slipping his hand around mine as I come even with him. The space is transformed. There are banners and fabric cleverly woven around the trees in bright flower-like colors that manage to feel seamless. A line of lanterns creates a path to the sacred spring, and the areas on either side are filled with sturdy wooden tables that will be filled to the brim with food and drink tonight.

The keep is filled to the bursting with guests who have traveled to celebrate with us. The first time it happened about four months after I arrived in this realm, I was overwhelmed and nearly had a breakdown, but now I enjoy all the new faces and business. I'll be happy when we're back to our normal number of people, but it's a nice change of pace.

I never get tired of feast days, though the preparation is exhausting. Doubly so now that I'm pregnant. The baby chooses that moment to kick, and I wince. "They're very strong."

"Of course they are. They have you for a mother." Sol loops an arm around my shoulders and tucks me against his side. We spent four lovely years with just him and me. It was the right choice to wait, to create a new life together with a strong foundation before we brought a baby into it. To give our people time to adjust to me the same way I needed time to adjust to my new role working with Aldis to conquer the ever-present paperwork that running a territory generates.

But, eventually, Sol and I decided together that we wanted to try to get pregnant. And the *trying* was some of the most fun I've ever had. I smile now to remember it.

When we first found out I was pregnant, he went into the pestering version of the mating frenzy. Every time I turned around, he was trying to bundle me up in blankets, carry me places, and feed me. Truthfully, he's barely relented in that care for the past nine months, even when I snarled at him. Maybe *especially* when I snarled at him.

I love my husband. Impossibly, that feeling seems to grow every day until I feel like I might burst with it. This whole life seems too good to be true sometimes.

"How did I get so lucky?"

Sol hisses lightly. "You say that like I'm not the lucky one."

The baby kicks again. I wince. "Speaking of our luck, the

little one will be born tomorrow in the middle of the celebration, with the way they're acting now."

"That is lucky, indeed." He gives me a careful squeeze. "A spring equinox baby is one born right as the seasons turn again. It's a fortunate birth."

"If you say so." I wander out from his arm, moving down the line of lanterns to the spring. I've descended those stone steps several times over the past five years. It's tempting to reach down and run my fingers along the surface, but in my current state, I'm just as likely to fall in head-first. My balance seems permanently altered with this pregnancy. It hasn't been a bad experience, but I won't pretend I'm not looking forward to a time when my body is my own again.

"Let's go back. If you want—"

"I do *not* need you to carry me." I take a step toward him and freeze as something warm and wet gushes down my legs. I can tell the moment Sol understands what happens because he goes so still, I'm not certain he's breathing. True fear rushes to the fore. My water just broke. The dragon midwife has talked me through this process time and again, arguing with Lenora, the human witch Ramanu showed up with one day. They don't agree on anything about this pregnancy and the inevitable birth…except that the babe will be born mostly human and develop more dragon-like features as they get older. That should be reassuring, but there hasn't been a dragon baby born by a human in generations.

"Sol, I need you to carry me back to the keep. Now."

He bursts into motion, sweeping me carefully up and sprinting back toward the keep. That's when the cramps that had been faintly plaguing me for what feels like days suddenly ramp up.

Sol practically kicks down the door, nearly taking out Lenora in the process. The dark-haired witch takes us in with wide eyes and then snaps at Sol, "Get her to the birthing room." She turns and starts roaring for the midwife.

* * *

THE LESS SAID about the birthing process, the better. There were moments when I thought it would last forever and moments when time passed too quickly. In some ways, it was easier for me than for Sol, because I was too focused on getting our child *out of me* to worry that I might not survive the event.

Several hours later, Lenora's dark hair was plastered to her sharp face as she snarled at me to *push one more time, Goddess damn it*. It was enough. My child was born just after midnight on the spring equinox.

Lucky girl.

Sometime later, Lenora and Birch, the dragon midwife, have slipped from the room, leaving Sol and I alone with our daughter. She's a strange little thing, all wrinkles and little hissing cries; as promised, she looks mostly human. When I first saw the blue tones, I thought she wasn't breathing. It was only when Sol thrust the baby close to my face that I realized the blue was actually little downy scales. Aldis says blue is a lucky color, one that's just as rare as my natural red hair in humans. Our daughter lies across my bare chest, silent at last as she sleeps.

I thought I knew love before. Terror. Protectiveness. It's nothing like what rises inside me now. I look up and meet Sol's gaze, seeing those feelings reflected in his dark eyes. A tear trickles out of the corner of my eye. "Tears really aren't only for sad times, are they?" I sniff. My voice is raspy and almost weak. "We did it. She's perfect."

"You both are." He smooths a hand across my temple. "Rest, Briar. I'll watch over you."

Exhaustion pulls at my eyelids, but I still manage to scoot over in the large bed and pat the space next to me. "Come here."

He edges into the space and then carefully gathers me and our daughter to him. His heat soaks through my tired body. It's almost enough to put me to sleep. But there's one last thing to do before I can rest. "What should we name her?"

It's an argument we've enjoyed having from the moment we found out I was pregnant. Occasionally words would get heated as we debated names, but we never landed on one that we both liked enough to short list it.

"I have an idea."

I don't have the strength to tense as his tentative tone. "Yes?"

"Hyacinth." He brushes a thumb over our baby's head. "It's the only flower we've found that grows in both realms. Not a rose, but—"

My chest goes tight and hot. "I love it." I wouldn't want her to be named Rose after my last name. No matter how happy I am now, it doesn't change that I left that part of me behind when I left the human realm. This is different, better. A way to honor both of her parents' origins. "Hyacinth," I whisper. "We have a great new world to show you."

* * *

THANK you so much for pre-ordering The Dragon's Bride! If you enjoyed it, please consider leaving a review.

Ready for more sexy good times in the demon realm? The Kraken's Sacrifice is next!

Catalina only made her deal with the demon because she had nowhere else to go. The world has kicked her every chance it got, so she's all too happy to

leave the realm she knows behind. What's the worst that could happen?

SHE DOESN'T ANTICIPATE BEING AUCTIONED AWAY to a *kraken*.

THANE IS COLD AND DISTANT...BUT he's not unkind. Isolated as they are, Catalina finds herself seeking his company again and again. And when she finally agrees to uphold her portion of the bargain?

THAT'S when things get *really* interesting.

BUT SHE ONLY GAVE THE demon seven years, and when the time is up, she'll have no choice but to leave behind the kraken who's stolen her heart and return to the world that doesn't want her.

Pre-Order The Kraken's Sacrifice!